I0654984

Playing with Matches

Lacey Schmidt

Playing with Matches

Lacey Schmidt

Affinity
Rainbow Publications

2017

Playing with Matches
© 2017 by Lacey Schmidt

Affinity E-Book Press NZ LTD
Canterbury, New Zealand

1st Edition

ISBN: 978-0-947528-86-7

All rights reserved.

No part of this book may be reproduced in any form without the express permission of the author and publisher. Please note that piracy of copyrighted materials violate the author's rights and is Illegal.

This is a work of fiction. Names, character, places, and incidents are the product of the author's imagination or are used fictitiously and any resemblance to actual persons living or dead, businesses, companies, events, or locales is entirely coincidental

Editor: CK King
Proof Editor: Alexis Smith
Cover Design: Irish Dragon Designs

Acknowledgments

Thank you to my soul mate, lovely wife, and caregiving hero, Laura. Thank you to my other perpetual heroes, Mom and Dad; and to my biological and acquired family for your love and support (without which writing would not happen)—especially my long-term, right-hand writing sister-in-crime, Carrie.

Thank you to the authors and women of Affinity.

Thank you to my brilliant and patient business partners for their continuous encouragement of my "second, secret career," writing fiction.

And last, but most of all, thank you for reading. I'm convinced we make the world a better place every time we read a book and expand our own inner world.

Dedication

To the people behind the people—the parents, siblings, children, spouses, and friends who love and support the caregivers, so we can keep giving care well, through disasters big and small.

And to Trey Garcia. We don't die, we just go out with our stereo on. I still hear you.

Table of Contents

Also by Lacey Schmidt

The Nightshade Lexicon

A Walk Away

Catch to Release

Love's Luck (Affinity Holiday Anthology

Chapter One

Social Credibility

Augusta Stuart was initially full of optimism and anticipation when her blind date, the ostensibly esteemed, local psychiatrist, Michelle Wynne, decided they should meet in person for the first time at the public library portal at the Briscoe Western Art Museum. Gus loved books, art, and history. And the more cautious side of her nature had also been pleased to discover the library was directly across the street from one of San Antonio's police stations. At the time, she never thought she would contemplate dashing into it before the first hour of their date was done.

She struggled to figure out where she had gone so wrong, as Michelle pushed her into a bathroom stall with a lascivious growl and pulled the stall door shut behind her. "Um. I just need to use the bathroom."

Michelle laughed and unbuttoned the top button of a silk shirt, exacerbating the severe plunge of its neckline. "Why Dr. Stuart, I didn't realize my psychological colleagues could be so shy of obvious attractions on first dates." She licked her lips suggestively. "We have so much in common, professionally, personally. Don't you think it's nice just to

1

unconsciously let go and act on our more physical impulses? It could be very nice. Right now, in fact." Her voice literally purred.

She was a beautiful woman. Voluptuous. Her hair was thick, straight, and incredibly lustrous in the florescent lighting. She scraped perfect teeth slowly over her berry-red bottom lip and eyed Gus provocatively.

Gus squirmed. "It's a restroom. We're in a public bathroom."

"Yes, we are." Michelle ran one finger down Gus's bare forearm, bringing goosebumps to the surface of her skin in the wake of her touch.

Breath accelerated, Gus eyed the walls of the stall and tried to collect her thoughts into some semblance of order.

Michelle leaned in and whispered hotly near her ear, "Are you afraid people will hear us and think less than charitable things about our propriety?"

The hairs on the back on Gus's neck stood at attention. She nodded.

"Hmm. Well, darling, you know it's not too healthy to worry about what others will think."

Gus shook her head, nodded, shook her head again. *That wasn't the point,* she thought, or maybe it was, but no, she was sure she had another point...

Michelle let out a loud throaty groan and several overtly excited *oh's* for emphasis. An amazing actress. Gus stood shocked and silent, unable to keep the abject horror out of her eyes.

Michelle laughed her great musical laugh and gave a coy smile. "See there, you're already guilty of it as far as every library patron can tell. We might as well make the most of it."

"I...I...uh..."

Michelle put one of Gus's hesitant hands on the swell of her breast. "You have something better to do?"

Gus stood frozen.

"We're both healthy, consenting adults. It's okay."

And that gave Gus the clarity she desperately needed. She withdrew her hand. "But that's just it. I'm sorry, Michelle, but I am not consenting."

"Ah." Michelle smiled sadly. "Looking for something a little slower?"

Gus nodded.

"Seems we're not the best match then." She unlocked the stall door and stepped back, allowing Gus some sight of freedom. "I can't say that I'm not disappointed. But of course, I respect your needs."

"Thank you," Gus whispered.

Michelle nodded and gave Gus another once over that Gus felt pretty sure should have incinerated the clothes clean off her body. "It was still a pleasure to meet you."

Politeness automated Gus's answer. "And you as well."

Michelle barked a laugh. "I'll let you go then. I'm guessing you do have better things to do." She waved and sashayed out the bathroom door, leaving Gus flummoxed in the stall.

"I do. I need to call home," she whispered to the now empty room. "And finish unpacking. And maybe rethink this online dating service idea."

†

"You did what?" June's thick Georgian drawl rose an octave at the end of her question.

Gus smiled at the incredulity in her older sister's tone. "I joined an online dating service called San Antonio Matches4All."

3

"What for?" June's skepticism was accompanied by the voices of her nephews' squabbling.

"Because I'm tired of being alone, but don't tell Mama that."

June laughed through her nose. "Yeah, we know her answer. She would tell you to quit trying to save the world and come back home to Atlanta where you're needed and loved. And you know what? I'm not so sure she isn't right."

"This is a good opportunity to use what I've spent the last decade learning and wanting to do, June. I can't give it up now."

"I get it. You want to help children. I even get that you want to help impoverished children, but I don't see why you can't do that here in Atlanta."

Gus squeezed her eyes shut and rubbed her forehead. "My chance to build a mental health service program for impoverished youth is here in San Antonio. I get to establish and direct the whole program from its start."

June snorted softly. "I think those two years with the Peace Corps in Guatemala turned you into a bleeding-heart liberal."

"You're one to talk. Besides, I think it was my fellowship at Harbor House that gave me the bleeding-heart and made Tyler Foundation interested in offering me this job."

"Your fluency with Spanish probably didn't hurt either." Her sister clicked her tongue.

Gus smiled. "Yeah."

"You know we're proud of you. I just worry about my baby sister, playing with matches online and all that."

"And Mama is putting the pressure on you to put the pressure on me, since July got engaged."

June gave a rolling laugh. "You know it, sister. Ever since our darling baby brother conned that sweet girl into marrying him, she's been telling me there is undeniable proof of miracles and asking how come it's so hard to find a wealthy, healthy lesbian to make her most educated daughter a wife."

"That's exactly why I signed up for the online dating site. I'm telling you all, it's impossible to find myself a wife if I never date—and you don't want me recruiting lesbians in bars."

"And they don't go to church?"

"Oh, sure. And you know the Catholic Church is so welcoming of gays these days; they've even taken to hosting lesbian socials in the most Catholic city in Texas."

"Now there is no reason to be so sarcastic with me, missy." June chuckled. "With that kind of obstinacy, it's no wonder we can't marry you off before you're an old maid."

"Well, that's probably a good part of the truth." Gus brushed aside a strand of her unruly, brown hair and gave a small sigh.

"Oh now, don't go getting all morose and moody on me now. You make friends with a fence post easy enough."

"Yeah, but it's hard being so far away from you all again. And if things work like I want them to here, that means I will remain far away from you all."

"You can always decide you've done enough and come home, Gus. It doesn't have to be forever, no matter how well it goes in San Antonio."

Gus twisted her cellphone charging chord around her index finger and let it loose again. "Yeah. You're right. I think I'm just P-M-S-ing on top of stressing over the move."

"You've done it before. You did fine for your two years in the Peace Corp in Guatemala, though Lord knows how many years in school, getting that fancy degree of yours, and even through your two years of fellowship in Nebraska for heaven's sake. You'll do fine in San Antonio, and we'll send care packages."

"Ooo." She anticipated the delicious goodies. "With some chocolate-covered goobers?"

"Sure, and some of my pecan pie cookies."

"You're the best."

"I know."

"Modest much?"

"Nah, my sister, the psychologist, told me too much humility damages my self-worth and ruins my social credibility."

"Blah, blah, blah. Your sister uses too much psychobabble."

"Yeah, she does. I love you, Gussie. I gotta go change your niece's diaper."

"I love you too, June. Kisses to all." Gus smiled, as she heard her newest niece, March, give a hearty squall.

June's reply was harried but warm. "And sugar back at ya. Bye, hon."

Chapter Two

Stuff Shrivels Up

A silken tongue hammered butterfly strokes over her tight, pulsing clitoris. Callia Alexana felt the waves of her orgasm mounting to crest over her entire body, tingling from the top of her head to the tips of her toes.

And then, her cherished, old alarm-clock radio sprang to life. A National Public Radio segment on Syria shattered her dream. She squeezed her eyes shut and tried to retain enough of the tattered remnants to achieve some relief, but the NPR segment ended and an announcer advertised one of her father's restaurant franchises, "Sponsored by Baba Alexana's Greek Deli." Her father's voice intoned an empathic, "Opah, good eats," for good measure, and she gave up the dream completely with a muttered curse and a sigh. *There are just some things you can't do for yourself, and that kind of oral pleasure is damn sure one of them*, she thought, as she lumbered out of bed and padded toward the shower. Saturday morning or not, she and Andy had some important logistics to work out if the Red Cross was going to have food and medical supplies for any of those Syrian refugees arriving in Caracas on Monday.

7

†

Nearly ten hours later, Cal squeezed her eyes shut and tried to ward off the headache building from the tensed muscles at the back of her neck.

"He doesn't give a rat's ass if we're bringing in medical supplies or not. No charter flights are allowed in from stateside, only boats." Andy tugged on his left ear and scowled. "Damn it, Cal, what else can we do?"

Cal paced, one long agitated leg in front of the other, in the small room like a wired panther. "He's going to have hundreds of families in need of medical attention in that bloody, back-assed, murder-happy hell hole." Cal slammed the meaty side of a closed fist against the closest wall before pacing back toward Andy's desk.

Andy grimaced.

Cal felt like she was at a breaking point. She could cuss like a sailor, but rarely did unless the anger bubbled up too hot and irrepressible. She knew she got that from her father. He appeared so mild mannered—like Clark Kent—or like baba ghanoush, the Levantine eggplant dish he was nicknamed after. He was calm and kind, ninety-five percent of the time, but if you ruffled, or heaven forbid, pulled on his feathers too much, then cuss words would fly out of him just like a chicken with Tourette syndrome.

"We'll have to use a boat," Andy suggested.

"Okay, I'll reroute the flight to San Juan, and we'll get that barefoot cruise skipper who motored supplies to Haiti last spring to move them on to Caracas... He's taken sanctioned dive trips to Venezuela before, right?"

"Yep." Andy smiled.

Cal thought about how good they were at this. No matter the red tape and hassles, it still felt good being adept at doing

8

something that helped. She worried though. Lately, it seemed like even the big wins didn't keep her smiling much. She dialed the skipper on her smartphone and negotiated the details with her shoulders thrown back and tried to keep her tone positive. She usually kept her hair short, so it stayed under her motorcycle helmet, but she had gone too long without a haircut again. A glossy, black strand fell forward along her jawline. She swiped it away with a frown and heard herself being no more than polite and quick with the skipper. She couldn't help but contrast her tone to when she'd spoken to the jovial skipper, Jeff, last spring. They'd traded banter and beer like baseball cards at a comic convention.

Sighing, Callia looked at Andy and announced, "Done."

Andy acknowledged her with a tilt of his head and finished bartering online with the charter flight service.

"I'll text Drs. Loftis and McPherson and let them know they'll have to meet the supply boat," Cal confirmed. She crumpled into an office chair nearby, with her fingers already wiggling over her phone screen. Fading daylight poured in the frosted, plate glass window of their office from the empty street outside, reminding Callia that it was approaching six o'clock on a beautiful spring evening. She glanced at Andy and found him looking back at her.

"Huron, Nik and Emily are grilling steaks. You know you're invited," Andy said.

Cal sighed. "I know."

"But?" Andy asked.

"Nothing. I'm just in the mood for a little downtime, alone, at home."

"Ah, must be a really big nothing if it is keeping you from hanging with Nik."

Cal loved all of them, but none so fiercely as her baby brother, Nikolai Alexana. Nik was even more of a black

9

sheep than his lesbian sister. He had appeared to follow the family hopes when he got his degree in culinary arts, much to the pride of their restaurant-mogul dad. Nik also married into the upper crust of San Antonio society when he fell in love with Huron Tyler's little sister, Emily. But Nik and Emily had promptly set up a low-scale, healthy-eating cafe that had no connection to Huron's grocery supply business or Baba Alexana's restaurant chains. They'd also set up shack in a one-bedroom renovated hotel apartment across from the county courthouse, shunning the empty Tyler mansion in Alamo Heights. While Nik, Emily, and Cal had always been a tight group, Cal thought their common opposition to the wills and wants of Huron Tyler and Baba Alexana over the last year had united them even more in their black sheep pack. She shoved her phone into the hip pocket of her jeans. "I saw Nik at lunch. He thought Emily would probably be late tonight, anyway. She's getting the new Harbor House facility ready for some psychologist they hired to build up the mental health clinic." Sarcasm slipped a more caustic edge into her tone than she intended. "And I can't really think of anything more fun than being the lone feminine sanity surrounded by you guys in the unchecked throes of your carnivorous testosterone."

Andy grimaced. "Hmm. On second thought, you're right. Can I come be solitary with you? I'm sure Huron will feel the need to talk about his latest exploits in bimbo land."

"Sorry, *vaquero*, you're on your own."

Grinning broadly, Andy put his hands behind his head and leaned back in his chair. "I'm not."

Cal cocked an eyebrow at him. "Andreas Arturo Pena, are you trying to intimate that one Miss Minola Jones has finally accepted your proposal?"

Andy gripped the armrests of his office chair and leaned forward. "I think so, Cal. I hope so. At least, Mina finally said she would think about it."

"When she said she'd think about it, did she also do that big buxom thing where she says," Callie inhaled a big breath and lowered her voice a register to imitate Mina's, "What's a *rico, suave* veteran want with an overweight, black woman and her two bastard children anyway?"

Andy shook his head. "No. She just said, 'I'll think on it sweet-cheeks,' and kissed me good-bye."

"Congratulations, Andy. I knew you would win her over."

"Persistence pays."

"Don't we know it." Callia smiled at him.

Andy blushed and blinked. "So when are you gonna go on a date again?"

Cal mock hissed, "Never."

"Aw, come on. You can't be abstinent forever. Stuff shrivels up."

"Ick, Andy. It does not. And nobody said I was abstinent."

"Now that's gross, Cal. Either you're getting physical with a girl you're ashamed to bring home to your family or…"

Cal studied the Saltillo tile floor and shook her head vaguely.

Andy continued, "Yeah, I know you're picky. So it's the other alternative, where you're secretly dating some fantastic woman who deserves to know your family and vice versa."

"Nah, neither." Cal felt the heat of a blush descend from the roots of her hair.

"Oh. TMI." Andy blinked.

"Right." Cal toed the tile.

"Anyway, my point is you should date, and you should just come out to Huron and your family."

"It's no secret."

"The hell it isn't. Have you ever said it out loud to any of them?" Andy gestured his concern with both hands.

"Yeah, I told Nik and Emily."

"That isn't what I'm asking and you know it."

"What good would it do to tell Baba out loud? What difference would it make? He would just go on plotting my life for me anyway. He's had me betrothed to Huron in his mind since we were knee-high on a grasshopper."

"Your father is stubborn, Cal, but he's a good man. I think he wants to see you happy more than he wants to see you do things his way."

"Bullshit. He can taste a Tyler-Alexana dynasty so clearly, he's already got a draft of a prenuptial operating agreement."

Andy shrugged. "I doubt it, but that still doesn't mean you should stay celibate. I mean that's like thwarting your nose to spite your face."

"No, my friend, that's reducing the complications I have to deal with for now. One day, I'll happen onto the woman who makes doing otherwise worth it, but I'm not gonna wrestle that fire-breathing dragon until I must."

"You know better. Just look at how long it took Mina to start to trust me. You don't seriously expect to bump into the right woman. You have to do some looking."

"There is no point in looking until my house is in order, so to speak."

"Yeah, so get your house in order, Callia Persephone Alexana."

Cal could tell he was excited now. The whole-name thing was something they only did to each other when they were serious. "Not now, Andy. Not yet. I'm not in the mood."

Andy frowned. "At this rate, you'll be older than dirt and the pickings will be slim by the time you're in the mood."

"Maybe. But not everyone gets true love anyway. There are other ways to be happy. See you *mañana*, stud." Cal picked up her motorcycle helmet and her skid jacket and walked for the door, leaving Andy to lock up the place.

Chapter Three

What Would don Quixote Do?

Gus sat on one of the piles of cardboard boxes spread around her tiny new living room and stared at her Converse sneakers. The sole on her left shoe had a blowout. Rubber flapped whenever she walked, and she couldn't even begin to remember which box labeled *office supplies* held the super glue or even which one had the rubber cement. She needed to find the box with her dress shoes, for that matter.

The sun was finally setting. It was still spring and it was already too hot in the afternoons for her pleasure. She stood up and shuffled across the newly buffed long-board floors of her rented duplex to the front screen door. The old house was small, but the inside was remodeled and clean. The bright, white walls and blonde wood floors felt cheery to her. A small central AC unit had even been included, and Gus was beyond-the-moon grateful. She stepped out onto the porch and pulled the old, wooden inner door shut to keep in the cooler air. The screen door gave a jovial tinny bang, as it shut behind her on its own automatic closing spring. She wanted to go for a walk and learn the neighborhood, but the flapping at her left heel reminded her that a stroll probably wasn't the best idea for a Zen moment right now.

A voice from behind her echoed her thoughts, "I don't think it's so safe to go out here at dark." Gus turned to find the speaker and noticed a boy of indeterminate age. He was too tall for ten years old, but too small and innocent appearing for fourteen. Maybe twelve years old.

"I'm Maverick," the boy said to the porch railing, his fingers picking at the new paint.

"I'm Gus. I just moved in here."

"Gus is a boy's name." Maverick looked her over with wide brown eyes.

"Yes, you're right. My whole name is Augusta. I was named after my grandmother, who was named after her dad, August. It is an old-fashioned name. Most people just call me Gus."

"People call me Mav. Or Martian," the boy offered.

"Nice to meet you, Mav."

No further response came forth. Watching the boy's polite but distant face, Gus suspected Mav might have what the diagnostic manual once called Asperger's syndrome. You could send the clinician home, she thought, but that didn't mean the clinician could leave the diagnostic tendencies at work. "Why do they call you Martian? Do you live next door?" Gus tried a broad gesture toward the door near hers, but Mav was still looking at the porch railing. She waited, thinking that the good Lord gave her plenty of patience, and patients. She smiled to herself at the old joke.

"I am going home, Gus. See you later." Mav slipped quickly along the porch railing, then along the front wall of the house and into the door beside her own.

Again, she thought he loitered somewhere on the autism spectrum. She pushed the thought away and tried to leave well enough alone for the evening, but she wasn't very good at it. She'd come here to help kids exactly like Mav.

She sighed and straightened her arms over her head, standing up onto her tiptoes until she felt her back give a satisfying pop. Tomorrow, she would start her first day as the supervising clinician at the Harbor House's brand new mental health services clinic for disadvantaged youth. "A supervising clinician in charge of myself alone at the moment," she whispered to herself and huffed out a breath.

She'd have to get the services started and wait for the board to find her the funding to staff up the place.

The press of trucks and SUVs parked along the curb on her narrow street made her realize that there was, no doubt, a certain car culture in San Antonio. For the umpteenth time since agreeing to take the job in south central Texas, she wondered if she should have bought a car. She'd never owned a car in her life. The youngest girl of six kids from a Georgia Cracker family, she knew plenty well how to survive without wheels. She'd tried out the bus route to the clinic twice already. It was a near straight shot, with only a few blocks' walk on each side, but the schedule was less than predictable from what she could tell. She thought it would be best to drag a change of clothes to stash in the office, in case she got too sweaty waiting out the bus on the way in—or missed it entirely and had to hike the two miles up St. Mary's Street to the renovated 1950s era shopping center that housed the clinic and it's football-field-sized gravel parking lot. She wondered how many of her patients would have cars and how many struggled to get from a home on the southern outskirts of town to work in the touristy hotspots downtown.

Her new clinic was set on the southern edges of downtown, convenient to the bus from the south-side neighborhoods. Census estimates indicated they would desperately need access to some kind of mental health services for youth. The dilapidated shops were in stark contrast to the pleasantly green and rustically tended grounds of the Tyler Grocery headquarters, directly across on Cesar Chavez Street. Obviously, the grocery distribution company did well.

A few blocks up from the clinic, Gus had discovered the Bexar County Courthouse and some other civic offices that could make the clinic more convenient for families traveling into the city center. Beyond the courthouse was a pretty square where Gus hoped to have time for an outdoor lunch or evening dinner, one day when the weather wasn't reminiscent of a glass-making furnace in operation.

She took a deep breath and wondered what changes the next six months would bring. The work she did over these next few months would determine if the clinic was worth having around. She knew that no matter how late she worked, no matter how much she scrapped and fought for resources, there would always be too many disadvantaged children and not enough mental health services to go around—but she wanted to make a dent. "I want to be don Quixote," she mumbled and fanned herself with one hand. "I just have to remember not to sacrifice so much of myself to the cause that I become a hollow, loveless husk. That's why I'm braving this Internet-dating bullshit. Surely, someone else out there is ready for a healthy, enduring, baggage-free romance."

Her self-pep talk fell short of inspiring any optimism. Intent on finding the box with her dress shoes before she went to bed, she trudged back inside as night slipped its cooler hands more thoroughly around the shrinking throat of daylight in the west.

Chapter Four

Murphy Shits on Everyone

The overcast sky put a lead-balloon ceiling over the world as far as Gus could see. Rain had threatened each day for the last two weeks. An empty threat. Street dogs spent most of the day barking in anticipation of a thunderstorm that would never come near her neighborhood. Summer storms in the Atlanta of Gus's childhood came over Lookout Mountain at a charge and let go for all they were worth. The squalls that rolled over the Nebraskan plains, where she'd interned with Boys Town, were much the same, and storms that blew over Guatemala during her Peace Corps days were often dreaded for how fast and long they let loose over the land. Texas held onto rain like an oblivious monarch taunting the peasants with cake. At first, she'd thought the overcast sky would be a relief from the oppressively bright heat, but the heat remained and the added humidity left her irritable at the sweat that constantly gathered underneath her hair.

The only benefit was that she could smell the water in the air. Gus looked up at the sky and gave a full sigh, as she stood, again, waiting for the bus.

A motorcycle sped around the corner and passed Gus in a huff of hot air. The loud engine gave a deafening rumble, as it carried its lithe, obviously female rider toward air conditioning. Even though Gus knew the rider must be hot and miserable under all that protective gear, she scowled her displeasure at the deafening decibels. "Future organ donor," she grumbled at the rider's graceful back, despite the spark of energy her libido got from the view.

†

The pale-skinned brown-haired woman waiting for the bus on the corner snagged Cal's attention, and she wasn't sure why. In those few sparse seconds, the air sizzled with something besides heat and humidity, but the traffic light turned green before Cal reached a stopping point. She didn't have time to look twice before she drove on to work.

Ignoring the threatening clouds that she knew from experience wouldn't produce any rain, she parked her motorcycle at the foot of the loading dock behind the old adobe-walled warehouse she had rehabilitated into the headquarters of MediXenia. Andy's Prius wasn't parked there yet, but she scanned the building's few windows for lights on anyway, knowing Andy sometimes walked the mile from his apartment. Only the security light showed. She keyed the fingerprint lock to the backdoor. The metal security door swung on well-oiled hinges and opened to the deeper silence of the positive-pressure building. The well-conditioned air tasted dry and clean, as she walked past the hurricane-proof steel and glass walls that defended their racks of dedicated, secure GPU servers. She rested easy in the knowledge everything was duplicated to a similar room in a bunker near Los Alamos.

"Murphy shits on everyone sooner or later," she whispered to herself, as she wandered into the kitchenette and started up the professional espresso machine retired from one of her father's restaurants. The pungent smell of perfectly roasted Kenyan AA coffee beans spoke directly to her cortex and almost brought an appreciative smile to her face. She placed her steel Yeti mug under the spigot and watched the black, liquid gold steam into it. "At least this always goes well." She patted the machine fondly, leaving it on for the others to use when they wandered in closer to eight o'clock. She took her steaming mug to the office she shared with Andy in the corner of the building.

It was dark, dry, and cool. As she stepped through the doorway the lights came on. Per habit, she rebooted both of her laptops and her desktop, then dropped into her ergonomic desk chair to wait for everything to fully cycle back on. She picked up the tennis ball to the left of her keyboard and proceeded to bounce the ball on the wall above her panel of monitors. Normally the routine helped clear her mind, but she found her thoughts straying further afield, back to the tatters of her last argument with her sister-in-law, Emily.

Only Andy, Em, and her brother Nik explicitly knew she was a lesbian. She didn't think there was any reason to point out the giant elephant in the room to the rest of her family, when they so obviously wanted to ignore it in preference of their dream that she would one day come to her senses and marry Emily's brother. Huron was her childhood friend and heir to the Tyler Grocery fortunes. Andy and Emily were becoming more persistent in their conviction that it was important to declare her sexuality, out loud, to the entire family. Cal knew it didn't matter though. Huron and her father would only see her sexual orientation as a minor obstacle to manage in their manipulations. She'd ruined her last and best chance at a relationship with her belief in that certainty, but she couldn't find it in herself to tell Andy, Emily, or Nik about that.

It had been over eighteen months since Jennifer Kim declared their almost relationship was officially finished. Cal remembered the resignation in Jen's dark, almond eyes, her beautifully broad-cheeked face smoothly determined not to give away any emotional dismay, as Jen explained she wanted out of the closet. The fact that Jen was closeted in the first place was what had made their relationship work so well. As a finance attorney for a very conservative, regional energy company and a first-generation Korean-American, Jen had as many reasons as Cal did to keep love, family, and work neatly compartmentalized. Keeping their affections on the down-low worked well for both of them, until Jen evolved. Cal loved her enough to let her go, knowing she would not make similar progress with her own family any time soon and that Jen would only come to resent her closeted role in Cal's life.

Telling Andy or Emily about Jen would only add fuel to their argument; and following their advice to bring home a girlfriend would only ignite an ugly cycle of denial, protest, and resentment among herself, Huron, and her father.

The panel of monitors in front of her came to life, as all systems came online. She caught the tennis ball's return from the wall one more time and set it aside. Shaking her head, she told the stillness around her, "And that is why I should just keep my problems to myself. No sense burdening friends and family with worries they can't fix."

A notification window from her voice mail popped up on her left-side monitor, indicating there was a voice message waiting from someone at the Red Cross regional office. Cal clicked play.

The treacle voice of the new Red Cross regional disaster response director slinked around the room as she hit play.

"Hello disaster service coordinators. This is your new regional executive director, Dan Argyle, calling to remind you about our next meeting in Austin. While we appreciate your long history as a volunteer, please remember that those who do not attend will not be allowed to continue volunteering. Also, please remember, I expect each coordinator to recruit at least two new corporate ready-when-the-time-comes sponsors before the end of the year. See you soon." Cal sneered as the canned recording concluded, and she remembered his smarmy leer over her the last time they spoke. That guy really gave her the heebie-jeebies, and she rued the day she didn't apply for the job herself—if only to avoid his leadership.

Cal clicked delete. "You're an ass wipe, Dan. Can't wait to endure you again."

"Good morning to you too, sunshine," Andy said as he entered the office.

†

Finally, Gus sat down at her desk, in the relief of the clinic's air conditioning. She took the opportunity before her first client appeared to go through both personal and work e-mails. With alarm, she viewed the two hundred and fifty-three notices from her San Antonio Matches4All profile and whispered, "Sweet Jesus. How the hell do I weed through so many?"

Chapter Five

Likely Narcissistic Personality Disorder

"How was your date with the gynecologist?" Gus's sister asked with evident glee.

"Horrible. Another dud. I'm starting to think this online dating schema is completely worthless."

"I told you," June said.

Gus clutched her cellphone tighter and rubbed her forehead. "Yeah, but you're not supposed to rub it in."

"So, what was wrong with the gynecologist, besides the weirdness of dating a woman who looks at a lot of other women's parts for a living?" Davis, June's husband, snorted in the background and said something Gus couldn't make out.

"She had fake, red nails long enough to be chopsticks and a laugh that was difficult to distinguish from a braying donkey. Plus, I'm pretty sure she went into medicine to facilitate her own hypochondriasis."

June laughed. "Well, at least she probably knew the difference between a psychologist and a psychiatrist and didn't ask you to prescribe any antidepressants like that copywriter, right?"

23

"There is that." Gus shuddered, as she remembered the copywriter with the startling underbite and wooly eyebrows.

"What about the artist?"

"She lives in a silo, literally, and thinks everyone should."

"Oh."

"Yeah."

"The physicist?"

"A Wiccan who reeked of cheap patchouli and cat pee. I sneezed for hours after ten minutes in her presence."

"How about the bank teller? Did you set up a meeting with her yet? Her profile picture is pretty hot."

Looking out her office window, Gus watched the sun flare orange as it started to sink beneath the broad expanse of live oak branches hanging over the edge of the center's empty parking lot. "I set something up for this Friday evening, but I got a package from her yesterday."

"You what? How'd she know where to send anything to you?" June's voice went up two octaves.

Gus scanned the parking lot again. "That is a very good question. She sent it to the center; so I'm guessing she had to do some online research to find out my last name and place of employment."

"That is a little disturbing, but I guess I might do something similar if I felt attracted to an online contact. What was in the package?"

"A gold bracelet with a diamond charm."

"Holy shit."

Gus chuckled. "Yeah. That's a pretty giant red flag."

"Yeah, so what are you gonna do?"

"I already repackaged it and mailed it back to the return address. I sent her an e-mail politely explaining that I thought it best we cancel Friday's date." Gus rolled her neck until she felt a helpful pop.

"Oh. How did that go?" A pot or pan clacked in the background as June spoke.

"She sent me back a five-page e-mail rant about how I was a controlling, manipulative bitch. I didn't respond. This morning, I got another two-page e-mail saying how sorry she was for her behavior and asking for a second chance to understand my needs."

"Whoa. Charming." Running water murmured beneath June's retort, and Gus pictured her sister cooking, with a baby on her hip and the phone pressed to her other ear.

"Mmm-mmm. Likely narcissistic personality disorder," Gus said.

"So the beautiful bank teller is out. What next?"

"I should get going, June. I'm still at work."

"Gus. It's almost eight o'clock your time. Why on earth are you still at work? Mamma would have your hide if she knew."

June's concern inspired Gus's first big smile in hours. "I know. I promise to be better tomorrow. There was just so much to do today, so many clients to see that I couldn't resist putting in a few extra hours."

"That is a good sign. At least your work ambitions are playing out well there."

"Don't worry, June, I haven't forgotten that I can come home anytime. I promise I will work out my romantic and social life too. I just need more time."

"Well, unlike Mamma, I'm okay if you take your time. I'd rather you make her more grandbabies with your soul mate."

"She would too, she's just worried my ovaries will be duds by the time I find said soul mate."

"There is that." June giggled.

"If I hurry out now I can catch the next bus home. I love you all."

"We love you too. July says to give him a call Sunday."

"I will. Good night, June."

"Good night, sister." June hung up, and Gus gathered her stuff together with one last look at the empty parking lot. She hoped the batty bank teller wouldn't decide to make any personal appearances after hours.

Chapter Six

High-Dollar Help at Bargain Basement Prices

"You wanna be careful with that. It'll peel the paint off your innards," a voice from behind advised, as Gus filled her cup with the life-giving coffee she'd so pleasantly discovered in the office kitchen that morning. Gus smiled and turned to find a very petite blonde woman with sky-blue eyes smiling up at her.

"Hi, I'm Emily Tyler-Alexana, and you must be Dr. Stuart?" The blonde asked, as she filled her own cup.

"Yes, I am. Please, call me Gus." Gus took a sip and let the caffeine roar its customary first, and most satisfactory, hello down her nerves. "And you would be *the* Mrs. Tyler-Alexana, as in the director of the Harbor House charity's board?"

Emily blushed and sighed over her own black coffee. "Yes, I am, but please call me Emily. I am also, and more importantly, your new administrative assistant."

Emily said it with a smile that hinted she was actually excited about being an administrative assistant in a way that she wasn't excited about directing the charity's board.

Gus gave her a half smile and replied, "I don't understand. Do you have a deep, inner need to personally handle medical records?"

"I checked the clinic's schedule, and I noticed the considerable client load you have already built up, Gus. I requested that the board find you an administrative assistant to manage scheduling and the record load, so that you're available to keep building more of the infrastructure this clinic needs. But it will take a few more weeks to actually make that happen." Emily shrugged, and the cascaded fabric of her beautiful bronze blouse shifted minutely. "The community has needed these services for so long, but we really didn't expect the clinic to take off so well, so quickly. I've got a business degree, and since we haven't yet raised sufficient funds or found a sufficiently qualified volunteer to support you, I thought I could fill the gap in the meantime. That is if you would like my help until we can afford to pay or guilt someone else into it?"

"Well, you are high-dollar help at bargain basement prices, Emily. How could I resist?"

Emily laughed, but kept both hands wrapped around her coffee cup and still looked a little uncertain of Gus's interest.

Gus raised her own mug in a vague gesture of cheers. "Yes, I would love your help and your ideas about how we might streamline things so that the clinic can offer more services to more families."

"I'm not sure I'll be all that much help, but I will try wholeheartedly." Emily's smile took up half her face, and her sincerity was palpable to Gus.

"I'm glad of the help, Emily. Just having someone to greet families and start in on the paperwork will be a big asset. That alone should save me twenty minutes a client."

"And maybe allow you to have a personal life too."

Gus was caught off guard by Emily's insight, and she realized her face must have shown her surprise. Emily's left hand, with a large, diamond ring, fluttered into a conciliatory gesture. "I just meant that based on all the long hours here alone, you probably haven't had much time for anything beyond sleeping, eating, and repeating."

"Ah."

"I meant no offense."

"None taken. Honestly, I'm not sure I want much personal time right now."

Emily's face fell into a frown, and her thin, blonde brows wiggled closer to a small, sudden crease above her pert nose. "Oh. Why? I mean, is everything okay? If you don't mind my asking."

"I don't mind. It's rare that anyone is brave enough to ask the psychologist that sort of question."

"I bet." Emily nodded.

"Well, I have to hurry to get ready for our first client of the day, but the brief story is that I joined an online dating service and it's been a teeny bit horrific so far."

"I can imagine."

"Thankfully, imagining is less horrific and probably as absurdly funny as experiencing it. I'll give you the highlights at lunch, if you're in for a good gossip over some of those banh mi sandwiches they make next door?"

"Deal." Both of Emily's hands were on her coffee cup again, but she was smiling and her sky-blue eyes twinkled with warmth.

Gus nodded, and as she headed for her office remarked, "Thank you, Emily. It's good to have your help, and it's even better to have a friend here."

Chapter Seven

Twelve Years with a Mexican Stripper

"I need a boring, average, content-with-things-in-their-place, accountant to date. Preferably, a good-looking accountant who handles all her own baggage and doesn't mind carrying mine for me from time to time." Gus muttered the small prayer under her breath.

She waited in the evening shade, glad that the sun was no longer glinting off the surrounding limestone facade of the little shops in La Villita. With kids still in school, La Villita was not yet overrun with tourists enamored of the Spanish colonial flavor of the "little village."

It reminded Gus of St. Augustine's old town area in Florida. She and her four sisters had once driven down Highway A1A in their dad's battered, old Buick with the steel bumpers, determined to see some of Florida's famous beaches and how the rich and famous lived. In that week, they'd eaten enough bologna sandwiches to last a life time. "What's for lunch? What's for dinner? What's for breakfast? Wanna snack?" the sisters sang, as they drove along with all the windows down, looking for a thirty-dollar room with a double bed and plenty of sleeping bag floor space to share.

Gus smiled at the memory. She was the youngest girl, fourteen at the time; and she felt so grown up and free, yet safe, in her pack of blonde sisters. They doted on Gus, with her dark-brown hair and brown eyes. She was the novel one and their baby sister, even after July appeared ten years later. Her dad called the girls his "breeding run" and July the "punctuation mark."

Gus sipped her lemon-ginger tea and missed her family. She acknowledged to herself that this probably wasn't the healthiest mindset to have at the start of a date, so she tried to think of something else while she waited.

She'd chosen La Villita based on Emily's recommendation that it was a safe place to meet a date, close to work, and easy to find. Gus and her blind date were both new to San Antonio. She had high hopes for this date. Sheila was a paramedic instructor in the navy and had just been transferred from San Diego to the new medical training facility at Fort Sam. Gus knew nothing about Fort Sam, she realized, other than the signs for the base along I35 on the drive into town. But they did share their exasperation with the opaque, even non-existent lesbian dating scene. During their e-mail exchanges, they'd agreed there didn't appear to be any social groups and there were no notices in the free papers for lesbian community centers and such. They had both discovered one long-standing gay bar, the Bonham Exchange near the Alamo, but found that was usually overrun with dancing boys and fag hags. It worried Gus, some, that these blind dates via SanAntonioMatches4All might actually be the easiest way to meet other lesbians and form a social network.

Her musings were interrupted when a heavily freckled blonde in a tank top, cargo pants, and combat boots pulled out her table's second chair and squeezed into it. Presumably, Sheila. The woman had biceps the size of Gus's thighs.

She smiled crookedly back at Gus and announced, "Yeah, I'm a top, and I'm a butch. So if that isn't your thing, then I guess we're going to be friends." Sheila's thigh-sized biceps bulged as she crossed her arms and rested back in her chair.

Gus was afraid Sheila's chair would prove too top heavy to balance on just two feeble legs on the old stone paving, but it held. She was glad, as she didn't really want to assess Sheila for a head injury before she finished her tea.

"We're going to be friends," Gus admitted. She didn't care so much one way or the other about the butch-versus-femme, top-versus-bottom debate, and she didn't feel any spark of attraction for Sheila.

"Well, damn. And I got all dressed up for this." Sheila frowned and then grinned with a shrug. "So what are you looking for, if you don't mind me asking?" she added after a few seconds of silence.

"Ah, mostly friends, and maybe a chance at dating."

"Shit. I can't stand dating." Sheila confessed, "I want someone beautiful to take home and enjoy. If there turns out to be enough enjoyment for everyone, then I'll do whatever I can to keep her in my bed. Sure you're not a tiny bit interested?" Sheila's hyper blonde eyebrows rose a little and her grin broadened.

Gus had to laugh. "Well, since you put it that way, um no, I don't think so." She smiled at the bold woman across from her. Sheila made the table look small. She was a blonde Viking warrior at a kindergarten tea party.

"Yeah, between you and me, I kind of a have a thing for women of color anyway," Sheila proclaimed.

Gus almost snorted her sip of tea out of her nose. The scent of lemon clove to the back of her mouth. "Why did you think that I was a woman of color?"

"I thought you spoke Spanish," Sheila admitted.

"Ah, I do. Fluently. Thanks to two years with the Peace Corps in Guatemala. Do you speak Spanish too?"

"Oh, yes, but thanks to twelve years of living with a Mexican stripper. I found her in a bar out near Miramar and took her home one long weekend. She quit stripping, got a green card, went to school, and learned to sound Californian. After twelve years, I came home one day and she said thanks and see ya. She'd gotten polished enough to attract the attention of a very wealthy corporate lawyer with a house in the hills overlooking Coronado Bay, so she was done with the likes of me."

Gus could see the real resentment still lurking behind Sheila's easygoing veneer. That one was still an open wound she thought, and she barely kept herself from openly scowling at the prospect of listening to another date bare a boatload of bad breakup baggage.

Sheila prattled on, "It was better anyway, Rena wouldn't have left San Diego with me when I was transferred. Things were probably cleaner this way. It was easier to decide what to do with the stuff she left behind. I just," she squinted into the distance over Gus's shoulder before continuing. "It just made me mad the way she left so easily, as if twelve years didn't build up a serious commitment at all. I know we never said we were married, but it isn't like either one of us dated anyone else in twelve years either. And suddenly, she's moving in with a woman she's never officially gone on a date with, or even gone home with, as far as I know. There had to be more going on than I knew about. I felt betrayed, you know? It takes a while to get back your trust after something like that. Does that make me weird?"

Gus took a deep breath, as she realized Sheila was looking to her for assurance. She knew that if she said Sheila was weird then Sheila would dismiss her as a quack. She also knew that if she said Sheila was normal, then Sheila would probably just dismiss Gus's opinion as polite non-sense whenever her insecurities sprang up again. Gus found herself wondering why she hadn't gone home and curled up on the couch with a book. "You're not weird. Most people feel betrayed at the end of a relationship, no matter who drives the conclusion of the relationship." Gus hated how her voice so easily slipped into psychologist mode.

Sheila frowned. "I don't see how Rena could have felt betrayed. She got everything she could possibly want. I came home every night. I spent every weekend with her that I wasn't working. She never wanted her own bike, just to ride bitch on mine, so I even got the rest bar put on back. She refused to wear a helmet and didn't want me to even wear mine because it got in her way of seeing stuff. It's true, I drew a line there. You know, being a paramedic, I'd seen too many head injuries. Granted, most motorcycle accidents rupture internal organs or snap spinal cords anyway, so the helmet isn't much good, but I'm damn sure not taking the chance of having an accident that leaves me a vegetable. Mangled would suck, but I could live with it. Drooling on myself with just enough brain cells to breathe would be too horrible."

At this last admission, Sheila's bare shoulders did shiver a tiny bit, even in the balmy evening. "But enough about that. You know, I didn't spring from the womb a liberated lesbian. I've got a fairly interesting coming out story I'd like to share with you. Would you tell me yours too?"

"Mine is pretty boring, but I would gladly tell you all about it," Gus said, as she rubbed at her temple with one hand. She was starting to get a headache, probably needed more water, but she couldn't force herself to look away from Sheila. It was too ingrained in her to devote all of her attention to anyone who was talking directly to her. She stayed focused on Sheila's dark eyes and found herself wondering if Sheila was really a blonde. Those eyebrows looked a little bleached.

Sheila nodded into the brief pause. "I'll go first. I'm originally from New Jersey. My parents were kind of old when they had me. They ran a kosher grocery store when I was little, but had retired before I started middle school. By high school, I was starting to suspect I liked the girlies. Much better than the boys." She leaned forward, and all four legs of her chair came back to the ground. "But I knew I wanted to see more of the world, too. I figured out I could travel for free if I joined the navy. Lots of girls joined through the medical corps. So, the fall of my senior year, when I turned eighteen I enlisted. There was one woman firefighter at the firehouse near us, and she was also a paramedic. I had a crush on her. So, when the recruiter asked me what I most wanted to do, I picked paramedics. The extra training required me to enlist for longer, but I didn't care. I was going to see the world and hang out with other paramedics who would probably all look like Donna down at the firehouse. I just had to figure out a way to tell my parents."

She paused for breath and then continued, "In my adolescent brilliance, I ended up just blurting out that I was a lesbian and had enlisted in the navy, at the dinner table one night. I thought being a lesbian would make my parents glad to be rid of me. Well, after about thirty seconds of silence, my mother started wailing. My father stood up and started pacing back and forth beside the table, yanking on his thin hair. It was a classic Jewish display of despair—just like I'd expected. I thought they'd be so upset over the lesbian thing that they wouldn't even really hear the navy part. And when they did remember, they'd be glad of that, at least. But I was wrong. My mother wrapped her arms around me, crying all over my head. Our dinners got cold while she went on and on about why did I need to break my poor mother's heart by leaving, only God knew where, for so long. My father added in bits about how they would surely be too old and dead before I could come back to them. Looking for any way out at that point, I strongly re-announced I was a lesbian and asked them if they weren't worried about that."

Sheila chuckled. "My mother just laughed. Why would she worry about a thing like that? Donna Zdarsky's mother had been worried, but look how well Donna turned out, working at the fire station and seeing her parents every week. My father just shrugged and said they had known about the lesbian thing for years. They just assumed I already knew they knew I was 'in the lifestyle,' as they put it." Sheila gave a big smile.

Despite her complete lack of physical attraction to Sheila, and her inability to get a word in edgewise with the woman, Gus found herself smiling back. "I could probably use a lesbian friend in this town, even if there isn't any chemistry between us."

Sheila gave her a knowing look. "Me too. Any chance you like beer? I know a great dive down the street."

"Absolutely. Can we walk there?"

Sheila stood up and loomed beside the table. "I don't see why not. It isn't like we could park any closer anyway." She gestured one large open hand toward the street and quirked an eyebrow. "Shall we?"

Chapter Eight

Borrowing Family

"So how was the date with the paramedic?" Emily handed Gus one of Nik's infamous jalapeno-basil margaritas on the rocks and sat down in the teakwood deck chair next to Gus.

Gus sipped her drink and let the sweet cool spice of lime and jalapeno sing through her insides for a few seconds before answering. "It reeked of mutually agreeable friendship possibilities."

"Hmm. Any friendship with benefits potential?"

"Nah. No physical attraction. No emotional sparks from either camp, you know?"

"Oh." Emily looked contemplative and fell silent.

Gus took another sip of her drink and felt the tequila loosening the tension in her neck muscles. The sunset lit the city sky beyond the rooftop of Nik and Emily's apartment building in a gradient of auburns and golds. The smell of beef, onions, and bell peppers on the grill attested to Nik's progress making fajitas.

Gus turned in her seat and held up her glass until she caught Nik's eye. "These are everything Emily promised and more, Nik. Thank you."

Nik held up his grilling tongs and gave a toothy grin. "You're welcome."

Gus thought he was a handsome man, and something about his easy smile spoke to how well his and Emily's sincerity and kindness matched. Between the two of them on their rooftop patio, she felt a sense of family and belonging, even if she knew it was only briefly borrowed.

The door on the west side of the patio flew open and knocked against the railing with a hearty thud. Gus squinted against the setting sun's sparkle, trying to make out who the newcomer might be before he spoke.

"Hey Nikolai! Good to see you, bubba. Where's my baby sister? I could use a hug." The deep-voiced newcomer was tall, blonde, well dressed, and reminded Gus of a GQ magazine cover model or a TV soap opera star. Nik was dark and handsome, but if a man could be said to be beautiful, this guy was it. She watched, as he patted Nik on the back and turned toward them at Nik's gesture.

Emily set her drink on the tile beneath her chair and bounded into his arms for a good squeezing. When Emily stepped back and smiled up at him, Gus recognized the family resemblance easily. Two blondes with blue eyes. Both pretty. She smiled to herself and wished she'd inherited those kinds of good looks.

He inclined his head toward Gus and asked Emily, "Now, will you properly introduce me to your friend?"

Emily spun in place to face Gus and gave a bright smile. "Gus, this is my brother, Huron Tyler. Huron, this is Augusta Stuart."

Gus startled as she put two and two together. Emily's brother was the chief owner and officer of Tyler Grocery

38

Supply, the charity's largest corporate sponsor and pretty much the main funding source of her new clinic. She set aside her drink and stood, briefly patting the side of her khaki skirt. She felt her right eye twitch, a nervous tick of hers, as she offered a smile. "Very pleased to meet you, Mr. Tyler."

His smiled widened further. "I assure you I am even more pleased to meet you, Dr. Stuart. Please, call me Huron." He darted a look of mock consternation toward Emily before continuing, "My dear baby sister has endlessly endorsed your professional qualifications, patience, and dedication to helping others, but she failed to mention your immense beauty." He briefly bowed his head and then looked up at her through thick lashes.

Gus felt the heat of a blush creeping up her neck. She touched the tip of her fingers to her breast bone to hide the rose glow she knew was now showing just beneath the hollow of her throat and forced herself to meet his twinkling blue eyes. "Why thank you. That is very flattering praise from a man as handsome and accomplished as yourself."

"Only the truth."

Emily cleared her throat. "We've started cocktail hour without you since you're late, and since Nik is already cooking, you will have to make your own if you care to join us."

"It's not like I'm the only one late. Where are Cal and Andy?" Huron's look of dejection and curiosity looked genuine.

"Who are Cal and Andy?" Gus asked.

Nik handed Huron an iced bottle of Shiner Bock. "See, I still made you a cocktail."

Huron grinned. "Thanks, brother."

Nik flipped a dark curl of hair out of his line of site as he looked to Gus. "Cal is my older sister and Huron's best friend. Andy is her business partner or partner in crime, depending on who you ask in my family."

"Oh, that sounds like several good stories," Gus replied.

"And I'd tell them all, too, since Cal and Andy are too busy to be here tonight, that is if I wasn't worried about burning the onions." Nik went back toward the grill with a grin. Gus decided his blue eyes were more electric looking than Huron's and hence the more appealing of the two, even if Nik wasn't half as fashionably good looking as Huron in general.

Dinner and sunset passed quickly in a content blur, and Gus found that polite charm infused Huron's social presence as well as it did Emily's. By the end of dinner, she had ceased thinking of him as a business magnate or funding source official of any sort. He was simply Emily's jovial, good looking, older brother.

"I promised to have Gus home no later than ten o'clock," Emily pointed out and picked up several dishes before heading toward the elevator.

"Right." Gus stood up and took an armload of dishes too. "Thank you for the lovely break, Nik. I'm no critic, but I'd rate you a five-star chef based on that meal alone."

"You know, I love cooking for hearty eaters. Definitely more than I like cooking for critics. You're welcome any time, Gus."

Huron stood up and placed his napkin on the table. "Hey Em, do you want me to drive Gus home on my way?"

Emily shook her head. "It's the opposite direction for you, Huron."

"Well, I don't mind if she doesn't." He directed a smile at Gus.

"She may not, but I would. We have some girl talk to do, and I planned on leaving you boys to yourselves."

Nik snorted. "She just wants you to stick around so I can get all the talk about sports and guns out of my system without boring her."

Huron shrugged. "I won't let my baby sister down then. You girls be careful." He sat back down.

Gus heard him ask, "Got any cigars?" as the elevator doors slid shut.

†

The inner-city streets were empty on a weeknight after dinner, and Emily's little Lexus was smooth and silent even on the older, bumpy streets as she drove Gus home.

Emily cruised to a stop at a red light. "You know, Gus, there is no way to say this without sounding meddlesome, so I'll just put it bluntly. I couldn't help but notice that you and Huron really get along. Is there any chance you'd be interested in dating my brother?"

Gus hadn't seen the proposal coming and was caught flat out. "Um. I mean...I...I'm..."

"I mean, I know you've put your faith in modern dating alternatives, online and all, and I'm not proposing you stop trying dates that way. I just thought that you might consider adding a date with Huron. You know, see how it goes kind of thing."

Gus ran back through all their chats about her dating escapades and realized she hadn't really specified anyone by name or gender, only profession. She knew a moment of fear, as she mentally tried and rejected several ways to tell Emily why a date with Huron wouldn't work for her.

Emily went on in the silence, "I promise, he doesn't have any direct input into the clinic's financing. There's no conflict of interest."

Gus raised her eyebrows.

"Well, there isn't any conflict of interest as far as Harbor House is concerned at least." Emily gave Gus a lopsided grin just before the light turned green and she eased the car forward.

Gus finally found her voice. "I'm not even in his league, Emily."

"What? Of course, you're in his league."

"No, I mean I'm not in the same dating circles, Emily. I'm a lesbian." Gus studied Emily's profile in the dim light trying to gauge her reaction.

"Oh."

"Is that a problem?" Gus asked softly.

"What?" Emily glanced at her quickly. "Hell no. It's not a problem, Gus. Not like that look says you're thinking it might be. I'm sorry. I just didn't realize, and I'm a little disappointed I can't recruit you as a sister-in-law."

Relieved, Gus giggled openly. "Yeah, that would have been really cool."

Chapter Nine

Denial Is a River that Runs Strong

"I've never, ever tried to set you up with anyone. Never. So, you know this is someone special, Cal." Emily frowned and Cal worked not to laugh. Emily was so sweet and petite that even when she was displeased it only reminded Cal of an angry squirrel or a wet kitten.

"I have no doubt she is, Em."

"Then what's the problem?"

"I'm not dating anyone."

"I know, and that is why Huron refuses to believe you're a lesbian."

"Huron would be in denial no matter what I did, and you know it. He's good at seeing the world exactly the way he wants it to be and that usually works for him. How he sees us is no different. Denial is a river that runs strong in Huron land."

Emily put her hands on her hips and shook her head. "Maybe so, but it would be a lot harder for him to dismiss the reasons you so persistently refuse his marriage proposals if you would explicitly tell your parents and get yourself a girlfriend."

"Oh, come on, Em. You know he would only entertain ideas of some glorious threesome and find some way to make it sound reasonable and legitimate enough for Baba to agree to some sort of marriage contract perpetuating it."

"I can't believe you would even..." Her angry-squirrel agitation notched up exponentially, so Cal decided to interrupt.

"Of course, I would dare say that, but only to you. As much as we love Huron, as much good as he accomplishes, we have no illusions about his playboy habits and motivations."

Emily shook her head and smiled briefly, sighing out some agitation in the process. "That's not what I can't believe you would say you thick twit."

"Oh."

"Yeah. I can't believe that you would deny your own ability to deny reality by deflecting to Huron's."

Cal tilted her head. Despite being a few years younger, Emily was always a guiding light in her life, but her advice and admonishments didn't usually come with a side of psychoanalysis. "I'm not denying anything. I'm being totally honest with myself and you. I do not want to date."

"Who does?" Emily retorted.

"What do you mean?"

"I mean that no one wants to date, Cal. It's scary, frequently awkward, and doesn't usually pan out."

"Says the woman who married her kindergarten sweetheart."

"Quit deflecting, damn it."

Cal snorted, "Yes, ma'am." She noted Emily's angry-squirrel demeanor was back in force.

"No one wants to date, but we all want a partner in life."

Cal thought about admitting that she didn't really think she wanted a partner in life. The pressure of disappointing someone else would always be present. Now, she just had to please herself, but telling Emily was probably a bad idea, so she kept silent.

Obviously, believing Cal was warming to her argument, Emily gave a small smile and patted Cal's shoulder. "And for most people, finding a soul mate involves dating."

Cal shrugged.

Emily sighed. "Just think about it for a while, Cal."

"Okay, I'll think about it." Cal realized she might have to suffer through one such date if she didn't want to face this same conversation with Emily every week for the next year.

Chapter Ten

Wry Vinnie's

Emily pulled the car into a choice spot in the empty parking lot of a slightly derelict building with a Chuck Berry aura, and Gus read the flickering neon sign, *Wry Vinnie's Rye Lounge*.

Gus asked, "Here?"

Emily's bright-blue eyes twinkled, and she undid her seatbelt. "Yes, here. They have the best martinis in town, at fabulous prices, and no tourists."

"But we're the only ones here." Gus looked pointedly around the parking lot.

Emily shrugged. "It's early. Besides, that means we'll have the place to ourselves and you can vent all you want."

Resigned, Gus undid her seatbelt, too, and slid out of the cool comfort of Emily's air conditioned Lexus. At five thirty in the afternoon, the San Antonio heat was at its flaming peak, and Gus's dark, heavy hair felt like a sweltering wool blanket on the back of her neck.

They crossed the short distance to the entrance, and Emily pulled open the heavy, red oak door. Gus nodded just to the left of the door, where a piece of battered, bright-green card stock proclaimed, *Vinnie never opens the lounge before six o'clock and always closes exactly one second past two in the morning.*

Emily smiled and pulled the door wider before ushering Gus in ahead of her. "Don't worry. Vinnie doesn't mind serving a few friends early."

The lounge's thin, red carpet barely cushioned their footsteps as they turned the corner into the dim lounge. A vacuum cleaner was switched on, and Gus spotted a dark-haired woman with swarthy skin in a sleeveless, red silk A-line and black patent Mary Janes pushing the hefty old machine. Abstract, art deco tattoos covered both of her bare arms, from wrist to shoulder. She looked up and noticed Gus with a frown. She switched off her vacuum with an irritable stare. "I'm sorry Miss, but we're not open until six."

Gus felt Emily gently push her aside as she stepped past. "Hi Vinnie, it's just me."

"Oh, Hello Em. It's good to see you." Vinnie's scowl turned into a bright smile, as she dropped the vacuum's cord and rushed to give Emily a hug.

After a good five-second count, their hug ended and they separated. Emily reached one hand back and squeezed Gus's forearm. "Vinnie, this is my friend, Augusta Stuart. Gus, this is Venetia Torres."

Vinnie offered Gus a smile. "Pleased to meet you."

Gus returned the smile. "Likewise. Emily has many great things to say about your famous martinis. I'm sorry we're early."

"Don't worry about it. I'm happy to make you two ladies the painkiller of your choice, so long as you don't mind the drone of my vacuum while you sip."

"We would put up with far worse in order to drink one of your martini's," Emily replied.

Vinnie bopped and twirled her way behind the bar, before pertly inquiring, "What will it be?"

"Make mine a double chocolate, please." Emily took a seat at one of the bar's sparkly pleather and chrome stools.

Gus mulled her request over, as she settled on a stool next to Emily. The pleather upholstery whispered a sticky squish against her dress slacks. She watched Vinnie top off Emily's double-chocolate martini with a dollop of whipped cream and a dark-chocolate swizzle stick.

Vinnie slid the drink carefully to Emily and said, "There you go. Just the way you like it, right?"

"Perfect. Thank you, Vinnie." Emily leaned toward the dainty looking martini glass and took a delicate sip without lifting it. A smidge of cream clung to her upper lip.

"How about you?" Vinnie asked Gus.

"Can you make one that tastes like sweet peach tea?"

Vinnie gave a toothy grin and nodded before delving around behind and under the bar for several minutes. She returned with a bottle of sweet-tea vodka and a thin bottle of peach limoncillo. The vodka was frosted over from being kept in the small freezer behind the bar. Vinnie twirled around again and came back with a similarly frosted martini glass. She poured two slugs of the vodka into a shaker, followed by a generous pour of the peach limoncello, and a dash of something from a small, unmarked brown bottle.

Gus kept the grimace off her face as she thought about how alcoholic this martini was going to taste.

Vinnie shook the mixer then let it sit, as she finished her magic by coating the rim of the frosted martini glass with some orange syrup and pink sugar crystals. She strained the mix into Gus's glass and pushed the pretty drink over to Gus. "Try it and tell me if I'm close."

Gus nodded, took a deep breath, and carefully lifted the glass to her lips. Only the smells of sugar, peach, and lemon greeted her. She took a tentative sip and the zing of the lemon hit first, followed by the sweetness of peach, and then the dry bite of sun-brewed tea. The drink was cold in her mouth, and she felt the tense muscles in her back inch loosen a bit. Surprised at how close the drink did resemble her mama's sweet peach tea, Gus set the glass back down on the bar with reverent care. "Wow, Vinnie. Just wow."

"Glad you like it." Her dark eyes glittered beneath the red glass pendulant light showering down on the bar's black surface. "I'm sorry to do this to you ladies, but I've got to get the vacuuming done before I officially open. I'll try to make it snappy." Vinnie spun her way from behind the bar, back to her vacuum, and made quick work of the lounge's thin carpet.

The volume of the old vacuum made talking impossible until Vinnie finished, so they sat in silence savoring their martinis.

Something about the taste of sweet peach tea always put Gus in that easy contemplative mood she found on the front porch of her parent's house, swinging as she watched the neighborhood's children shriek up and down the hillside street on their bicycles and skateboards.

She snuck a glance at Emily and found her looking similarly dreamy and staring distantly at the mirror behind the bar. Content that Emily wouldn't be offended, Gus let her mind wander afield.

Vinnie's vacuum came to a halt.

Emily nudged Gus's elbow with her own. "So Doc, what's up? Or more specifically what's got you down?"

Gus blinked. "Hey, that's my role."

Emily shrugged. "Someone has to shrink the shrink, right?"

"Technically, a psychiatrist is a shrink. I'm a psychologist."

"Quit dodging the question, Doc."

Gus smiled. "Tough crowd."

"Yeah, well, it's obvious something has you down."

"You mean besides the normal overwhelming fear that we're trying to help families so needy that most of their homes are cardboard box add-ons to their cousin's cinderblock shanties?"

"Yeah, besides that. You're used to that." Emily sipped her martini but somehow still managed to keep eye contact with Gus over the broad rim of her glass.

Gus felt herself blush. "Well, I guess it's all these online dating misadventures."

"Yeah? How is it going lately?"

"I've gone on dozens of dates."

"You must be making lots of friends."

"Sort of, but that isn't really the point. You know?"

Emily's eyebrows knotted. "Um. No, I'm not sure I do know. Tell me more. What's the point?"

"I guess, I just hoped for a more meaningful connection. I thought it would take a lot less dates to connect with someone I might be able to share important things with one day. Like my hopes, and fears."

"And stressors?" Emily smiled.

"Yeah. But even more so, someone who didn't need more psychological support than they could give. An intellectual and emotional partner. Does that make sense?" Gus took a long sip from her martini.

"Sure. Makes sense to me. I'm married to a true intellectual and emotional partner. I hope everyone has that opportunity."

"Yeah, well so far, San Antonio Matches4All has been a letdown as far as leads on finding anyone like that."

"I won't say I told you so."

Gus laughed. "You just did."

"You noticed." Emily winked and set her empty glass on the bar. "I will say what you need is someone to set you up with a known entity. Someone who knows something about you and what you value in a relationship."

"A matchmaker?"

"Yeah."

"I don't know. I mean what if I'm just difficult to get along with and anyone setting up dates for me is just doomed to frustration?"

"You're easy to get along with. I don't think that part would be a problem."

"Well, I don't know anyone well enough to ask for that kind of favor anyway."

"You know me well enough."

"You would be willing to set me up on a date with someone you know?" Gus tried to keep the hopefulness from cracking her voice.

"Would you really be willing to go on a date with someone I thought would be a good match?" Emily bit her lip and twisted on her bar stool to face Gus more directly.

"Yes. I think I would. At least you know me face to face, as a whole person, and not just a profile. And I know you enough to know you have generally good intentions toward everyone you meet."

"But there is a disclaimer."

Gus tilted her head and looked into Emily's concerned blue eyes. "What's that?"

"Even with good intentions, I might be wrong, and the results might be bad."

"You don't want me to hold you responsible if it doesn't work out," Gus guessed.

"Sort of. I mean, I may be responsible, at least partly in some way. I would never say I have no responsibility for the results, but I don't want to risk losing a friend or the clinic's director." Emily twisted her hands.

"If I don't like the results, I promise not to hold a grudge against you for trying to help me. More importantly, I promise to remember I am entirely responsible for my own actions and reactions to other people." Gus reached out and gave Emily's clasped hands a squeeze. "I don't want to lose my friend either."

Nodding, Emily let out a breathy, "Okay."

"Did you have someone in mind?" Gus played with the napkin under her martini.

Chapter Eleven

Dating Blinders

Cal squeezed her motorcycle between the tightly parked cars into an empty spot behind the dumpster. Even the twilight hour was sweltering now, and Cal gladly took off her helmet. She locked it to the cycle's handlebars with a well-practiced click before rushing her fingers through her hair to straighten out her stacked bob with the aid of a rearview mirror. She spoke to her reflection, "Em thinks the world of her, so it's worth looking good." After a second of scrounging in the outer pocket of her ballistic-mesh jacket, she found the face-toning wipe she'd stashed there earlier. She cleaned the sweat carefully from her face and neck, then tossed the wipe and its wrapper into the dumpster.

Cal glared at the large, purple-black grackle that descended from the diner's roof to get a closer look at her custom-built café racer. "Don't get any ideas."

The bird chirped and hopped backward three paces.

"Right. Thanks. Here goes nothing then." Cal sighed. "Wish me luck."

The bird gave her a wide, yellow-eyed look, but said nothing in reply.

She forced herself to march around the building toward her blind-date destiny. The sunset patio in front of the diner was hustling, but she knew Emily had already made the reservation for two and had the table held. Walking on, Cal noted a woman sitting alone at a bistro table near the end of the row facing Lavaca Street, just where Emily had told them to meet. From fifty feet away, Augusta Stuart's profile was in clear view, and her beauty set Cal's knees knocking. She stopped in her tracks and took several deep breaths, letting them go slowly. She wiped her sweaty hands on the backside of her jeans and focused on taking stock of Dr. Stuart instead of doubting herself.

Dr. Stuart wore her long, dark, wavy hair loosely tied back in a half chignon that showed off her heart-shaped face, aquiline nose, and slender neck to crippling effect. The small bistro chairs looked sized to fit her, as she sat watching the traffic in khaki capris and a white pin-tuck shirt. "Em was right. Everything about this woman is classic." Cal looked over her own blue jeans, glad she'd chosen the dark blue ones to go with one of her more expensive marled, red t-shirts. She fixed a smile on her face and stepped forward.

Unfortunately, she stepped forward right into a downward spiral of bird crap. A damp wad of ammonia reeking filth plastered her left shoulder, settling through the mesh of her motorcycle jacket onto her red t-shirt with disturbing clarity.

"Well, shit." Cal's pulse tripled, as she tried to reason herself out of murdering the closest bird. A bright-eyed teenaged busboy noticed her dilemma and came running to her aid with a clean, damp bar towel, but as he reached out to offer her the towel a back-peddling man in a brown business suit bumped into both of them. The weight of the bump caught Cal off balance, and she fell sideways into the middle of a bistro table. Unable to catch herself, she sent the table crashing to the ground beneath her, and two twenty-four-ounce glasses of ale toppled all over her jeans.

"Oh my, are you, all right?" asked one of the table's occupants, a Hispanic man in a straw fedora.

The busboy offered her a trembling hand up.

"I'm fine. Thanks." Cal answered, as she untangled herself from the table's squelching, clinking grasp and stood up. "I'm afraid your table and your drinks are not though." Cal didn't dare look around to see how many people had noticed, or if Dr. Stuart was looking on.

"Don't worry about the table. I'll get another one from the back," the busboy said before rushing off.

Cal turned toward the man in the fedora. "I'll buy you another round."

Tanned lines bracketed the man's smile. "No, no need. I noticed your fall was helped along. We're just glad you're okay."

"Thanks." Cal nodded. She turned on her heal and made a beeline for the bathrooms. No matter what, she would stink of beer and bird shit, but she did what she could with a harried five minutes in front of the sink with a dozen paper towels and pink powdered soap. Seven women washed their hands next to her as she worked, only two gave her any sideways glances.

†

Gus checked her watch again before turning her gaze back toward the street and her thoughts back to her more challenging patients.

"Dr. Stuart?" The voice that interrupted her thoughts was like honeyed whisky, smooth and a little low, golden warm tones, with a precise bite at the end. The slight hint of that broad Texas accent twanged beneath the words. She turned her head toward the source. "Yes?" Her gaze met dark, blue-grey eyes and a shiver traveled between her shoulder blades.

Those arresting eyes drifted away from Gus's gaze, down to the empty chair at her table. "Hi. I'm Callia Alexana."

As Callia extended her hand, a wailing siren went off and she patted the pocket of her jacket. Her thin, olive-skinned face and high cheek bones flamed red, and her brows furrowed. She reached a hand into her pocket and pulled out a platinum-cased smartphone. After several seconds of perusing the phone's screen and tapping it a bit, she finally stuffed the phone back in its pocket and sat down.

A strong waft of stale beer greeted Gus, as Callia pulled the chair closer to the table.

Gus peered through the dim twilight lighting her blind date, trying to ascertain if she was already several pints ahead. Had Nik's sister spent the whole day in a sports bar?

Callia cleared her throat. "Anyway, you can call me Cal if you like. It's nice to meet you Dr. Stuart." Her V-neck t-shirt left her throat well exposed, and Gus could see her swallow.

"Please, call me Gus." Those dark eyes met hers again as she replied. Gus smiled, but Callia did not smile back.

"Gus?" The left side of Callia's wide, lush lips turned downward.

Gus felt like cold water was poured all over her initial attraction to Nik's sister, as she realized the specter of disapproval in that gaze. She struggled to keep the defensive tightness out of her reply. "Yes, Gus. One syllable. Short for Augusta."

Callia licked her lips and leaned forward. "What kind of name is Augusta?"

Gus scowled before she could stop herself. "What kind of name is Callia?"

Callia blinked. "Um. Greek. My family is half German, half Greek. My dad picked it because it was like a flower, and my mom had already named my two older brothers, Hans and Coen, after her Germanic ancestors."

Gus relaxed her shoulders and considered that maybe the woman just wasn't suave, despite her smooth, techno-brat appearance and level tone of voice. "Oh, well it is pretty like a flower."

Callia smirked. "Yeah, thanks. That's just how I feel. Pretty. Like a flower." Her tone dripped sarcasm thicker than unfiltered honey.

More like a prickly cactus, Gus thought and looked back for a server to help speed things along. She laid her hands flat on the table in front of her and held in her sigh.

"So what kind of name is Gus?" Callia tapped two fingers lightly on top of Gus's hand on the table.

Gus made eye contact with her again, and the skin on the back of her hand warmed with the brush of Callia's fingertips. Gus bit her lip.

Callia gave a tentative smile.

"French maybe." Gus shrugged. "I was named after my grandmother, or rather, I was named for the month I was born in like my grandmother, who was also born in August. It's an old family tradition."

The smooth skin between Callia's eyebrows creased again. "Really? You're not kidding me?"

Gus lowered her head. "Yes. Really. I have four older sisters, June, May, April and Deci for December. And one younger brother, July."

"Holy cow." Callia blew out a comical sigh. The street lights came on along the sidewalk beside their table.

Gus grit her teeth and thought it was great how Murphy's law worked so well for her like this—finally, a woman she was physically attracted to and who already had a legitimate connection to her life, and that woman only managed to raise her hackles.

A server placed two menus down on the table. "Can I get you ladies anything to drink?"

"I'd like a water, please," Gus replied.

"I'll try the Guadalupe Cream Ale," Callia said.

Again, the whiff of beer greeted Gus, as Callia picked up her menu and shifted in her chair. "Haven't you had enough?" The words escaped Gus, as she worried about how long she would have to wait through this awkward date before she felt it was safe to put her date on the road again.

Callia growled, "Excuse me?"

Gus sighed and rubbed the space between her eyes where her headache was intensifying. "I'm sorry, it's just that you reek of beer already; you were fifteen minutes late; you're obviously bored or uncomfortable or something, and this isn't going well is it?"

For a brief second, in the roaring silence that followed her admission, Gus could see a flicker of surprised pain in Callia's eyes. "I—it—no."

Then those blue-grey eyes became a colder, bolder shade of grey, and Callia's face closed out all emotions. "No sense in putting us both through any more awkwardness. Feel free to go. I'll close the tab." Callia shoulders visibly stiffened, as she canted her lean form into a straighter posture and inspected her fingernails.

Gus's ears grew flaming hot. "Right. Okay then." Something that felt as bulky and bland as regret settled hard in her stomach as Gus stood up. "I'm sorry."

"Don't worry about it." Callia waved her off.

As she threaded her way through the crowd and down the street toward the bus stop, the seeds of a stress migraine started to blossom behind Gus's eyes. She rode the bus home hoping their disaster of a date wouldn't disappoint Nik and Emily too much.

Later, in the dark of her bedroom, with all the curtains pulled tight and the air conditioning on full force, the honeyed sound of Callia Alexana saying her name echoed in a loop lulling Gus to sleep.

Chapter Twelve

Fanning the Flames

"It's like playing with matches," Andy told Emily as they sat at a corner table in a *panaderia* near the clinic, wolfing down the avocado torta special.

Emily tilted her pert chin and raised her fine, blonde eyebrows at him. "How so?"

"You know you're going to get burned, or at least you think you are, but you can't resist creating that warm, pretty flare anyway." Andy grinned. "I think Cal is attracted to your Dr. Stuart just like that."

Emily shook her head. "Gus isn't the type to burn anyone." A bell rang as another customer entered the bakery and joined the throng waiting to order at the counter.

"Maybe not, but that's not what I really meant. It's more that Cal thinks getting close to anyone will get her burned. She would have to come clean with Baba about her sexuality if it lasted too long, or risk losing whatever flame she kindled when her lover got tired of being an invisible elephant in the room. And from what she says of Dr. Stuart, that woman burns too bright to hide."

"You have a point there. Gus is all ethics and not afraid to shine. But she is also a psychologist. I've seen her exhibit patience and kindness with some very frustrating characters of a whole lot less obvious worth than Cal."

Andy finished off his sandwich, wiped his hands with a flimsy paper napkin, and cracked his knuckles. "Do you think that she is attracted enough to Cal to put up with the crap?" He sipped his cold Coke and waited as Emily considered.

"I think her eyes were blazing with denied attraction the whole time she was telling me about their disaster of a date." Emily nodded. "She talked about their date in a lot more detail than any of her others. Like, she even noticed how Cal smelled and exactly what she was wearing."

"Yeah, Cal seemed to have the same sort of reaction. She spent a whole lot of words describing how Dr. Stuart looked and why dating her was obviously a bad idea. Cal went on and on about how she was too prude, even after I assured her I believed her."

Emily smiled. "She was convincing herself."

"Trying to anyways." Andy nodded. "Do you think Dr. Stuart has enough patience to chew through Cal's bitter exterior to the sweet crunchy center?"

Emily shrugged. "Only one way to find out, right?" She pushed her plate toward Andy. "Do you want the rest of mine?"

"Hmm." Andy took the sandwich and thought it over, as he finished off Emily's lunch.

Emily leaned back from the table. "Maybe it is a bit like playing with matches. We might make either or both of them angry by interfering, but if we do nothing, they may miss out on their best chance to spark a real love."

Andy wiped his hands clean on another pitiful napkin. "Yeah, well, I guess. You're ever the optimist, Em, but I do agree that we should try to do something, so long as we don't get burned. Cal can't get so angry that she cuts us out of her life. That would definitely leave her without any spark."

Emily's eyes opened wider. "Yeah, I think you're right. Gus, too. She's used to having a big, warm loving family close by, interfering with her life, but I don't think she has anyone in that role nearby, right now. I worry we'd lose her back to her family in Atlanta if I burned too much goodwill setting them up again."

"We need to do something subtle then."

"Right."

"Got any ideas?"

Emily smiled. "Maybe."

"I'm all ears."

"Are you and Cal still heading to that regional Red Cross coordination meeting in Austin next week?" Emily rubbed her hands together.

Nodding, Andy licked his lips.

Playing with Matches

Chapter Thirteen

Red Crossed

"Is this the right Sadie Street?" Andy asked, as he threaded his Prius through the Lavaca neighborhood.

Cal sat with her socked feet on the dashboard, empty boots on the floorboard. "Yep. Em said she lived within a few miles of the clinic."

"I understand getting to know the population you serve, but surely, she could live some place just a tad safer."

"Ah, this neighborhood isn't so bad. It's historic, and Baba still owns a deli on the southern edge, so some of the residents must have enough money to eat out."

"Well, that's reassuring." Andy scanned the few addresses still legibly featured on some of the houses.

"208A Sadie. There it is." Cal pointed to a bright-teal house with two front doors.

The whole place looked big enough to hold at least four gnats, as far as Andy was concerned. The good news was that the lime-washed front porch was at least as big as the house itself. The door of apartment A was clearly marked with an electrical tape outline of the letter. He pulled his

Prius into the empty, cracked-concrete drive. "It doesn't look like anyone's home."

"Well, she doesn't own a car, or she wouldn't need the ride, right?" Cal backhanded him on the shoulder. "I'll go ring the bell, my manly man."

"Cheerio. I'll stay with the car, mum."

Cal shoved her feet into her boots and popped out of the car.

Andy watched her go and crossed his fingers. "At least she's starting out in a good mood." He watched Cal bounce across the porch, pull open the battered screen door, and rap her knuckles on the front door.

A petite woman with dark, wavy, shoulder-length hair in a butter-colored shift opened the door with a smile, and Andy caught his first live glimpse of Augusta Stuart. He couldn't put his finger on exactly why, but he realized she was stunning. It wasn't any particularly striking feature. She was a compact woman with average curves, brown hair, brown eyes, and smooth but otherwise unremarkable skin. On paper, she would probably read as plain looking, but in the Technicolor, real world, he admitted she was incredibly well made. Easy to look at.

As she and Cal approached the car, she smiled at him through the windshield, and golden tones lit her brown eyes.

Cal opened the front passenger door and gestured Gus should take the seat, before she opened the back door and slid in herself.

"Hi, I'm Andy and you must be Gus." He held his hand out to greet her, after she clicked her seatbelt in place and closed the door. The smile she gave him could have single-handedly thawed out Shackleton's frozen Antarctic expedition. He felt himself returning that smile, as she placed her smaller, cool hand in his and shook it with a firm but gentle grip.

"Hi, Andy. It's a pleasure to meet you in person, finally. I've heard so many good things about you from Emily and Nik."

"Most of which is probably, partially true," Cal interjected.

"Don't mind her. All the good stuff is obviously true. It's the bad that's only partially true." Andy released Gus's hand and focused on backing the car out of the driveway.

"We've got extra pecan crunch granola bars, if you missed breakfast." Cal offered from the back seat.

Gus laughed, and Cal leaned forward and shot Andy a quizzical glance in the rearview. "What? What's so funny?"

"I'm sorry. It just cracks me up every time I hear a Texan say puh-con," Gus answered.

Andy was a little shocked that the demure clinician was so readily willing to tease Cal, especially after their purportedly disastrous first encounter, but more shocking was that Cal actually giggled. She drew out the word for Gus three more times. "Puh-con. puh-con. puh-con. Yeah, it does sound dumb, but it still sounds more like something I'd want to eat than when you say pee-can."

"Oh my." Gus laughed again. "I never thought how that sounded."

"Yeah, but your southern drawl is nice otherwise," Cal said and leaned back in her seat. "I take it that means you don't need a granola bar though?"

"No, thank you. I've had breakfast."

"I hope you can find room for second breakfast," Andy said, as he gassed the Prius to accelerate up the short on-ramp for the interstate to Austin.

"Why is that?" Gus asked.

He and Cal nearly sung in unison, "Because we're stopping at Tenayuca's for breakfast tacos and beef jerky."

Their subsequent laughter reverberated around the car's interior, before Gus was able to ask, "What's Tenayuca's?"

"Technically, it's a gas station halfway between here and our meeting. But more precisely, it's an awesome fifty-year-old taco shop masquerading as a gas station, with lots of clean toilets," Cal replied.

"Okay. Why masquerade as a gas station?"

"It gets people to stop the first time, I guess. After that, the smell of tacos keeps them coming back whether they need fuel or not," Andy explained.

"There is probably a bad joke in there somewhere about bean and cheese tacos and gas," Cal remarked.

"Indeed." The one word Gus uttered came out as a tease.

"Can't help yourself can you, Cal?" Andy shook his head.

"It's part of my pert persona," she retorted.

"Oh, is that what you call it, boss?"

"Slight change of subject," Gus interrupted their banter.

"Sounds good," Andy encouraged her to go on.

"Tell me more about the company that you two run. MediXenia, right?"

Andy decided to let Cal answer.

"We use health data analytics and cloud-based technology to facilitate better revenue cycle management and logistics for healthcare organizations and emergency management services."

"Mmm. I think I understand what that might mean, but I have to admit I'm not very business minded. Can you give me some examples?" Gus asked.

Andy could hear the excitement in Cal's voice as she replied, "Sure. We do descriptive and predictive modeling of things like how many clinics a hospital should open in order to provide services to all the people wanting access, while still realizing enough profit to sustain the operations of those clinics over the long term. And we offer, to both private and public emergency services, cloud-based platforms for optimizing emergency preparedness and disaster response. We provide real time, non-invasive, reimbursement tracking and stocking systems, so that they don't have to spend so much time on administrative and logistics tasks while they're already busy with a critical medical situation."

"Oh. Cool," Gus replied, her voice perky and reassuring despite the vagueness of her reply.

Andy sighed, shook his head and smiled. "Cal is a genius, but she's crap at explaining what we do in a way that anyone cares about."

"Let's hear you do any better," Cal grumbled.

"I will. Here's the sixty-second, elevator pitch, Gus. MediXenia makes sure healthcare providers are free to practice the compassionate medicine patients and family really value by taking the devil out of the management details."

"That's vague and kind of misleading," Cal protested.

"It's a simple explanation, Cal. Once a person is interested and willing to hear more, then you can tell them the how."

"I do understand a lot better now," Gus supported him.

Andy grinned and flicked his eyebrows at Cal in the rearview mirror. He was startled to find her glowering at the back of his seat and surmised she wanted to look good for Gus—a sure sign she cared more about the psychologist's opinion than she cared to admit.

He cleared his throat. "Well, what Cal isn't telling you is that it's her business. She's the founder, the brains, and the grit behind it all."

"You're a part owner now," Cal protested.

"I am, but only because you insisted on making that part of my hiring package. My ownership would have been a worthless perk if you hadn't already made the company so financially viable on your own. You should take credit where it's due, my friend. You made this."

He checked her in the rearview mirror again and found her tongue-tied, avoiding eye contact, and with a slight blush warming the olive-toned skin over her high cheekbones. He glanced at Gus, and she caught his gaze with a smile before turning her face toward Cal.

"So, Emily's idea of creating a list of developments we want for our clinics, prioritized by their impact and the amount of effort required to put them in place, and then storing it on the cloud came from y'all, didn't it?" The admiration was apparent in her voice.

Andy shrugged, knowing Emily could have picked it up from dinner conversations, but Cal was quick to answer, "It's part of our standard advice, but applying it to your clinics was all Em's doing."

"Well, it's a great idea. Thank you for inspiring Emily."

"Thank you. We're happy to help," Andy answered, because he knew Cal frequently forgot the basic pleasantries.

"In that case, I'm happy to take advantage of your help. Records management is a real challenge, but I don't want to spend a lot of money on an expensive system or application so early in the clinic's lifespan, when I'm not sure what will wear well over time."

"And you don't want to wait too long to pick a long-term system and then have to spend a lot of time exporting records either." Cal was obviously excited to talk about something in her practical domain of expertise.

"Before you two begin boring the driver, I think you should wait to talk shop until after we've had tacos." Andy pulled the Prius off at the exit for Tenayuca's, feeling pleased with himself and Emily's plan for them to ride share. It was going so well, he speculated that before they returned home, the women would be flirting as if that first blind date had never even happened. Tasty tacos could only make everyone that much happier.

†

They walked into the meeting a few minutes early and full of tacos. Cal was feeling unexpectedly content after the pleasant ride in with Gus and Andy. She suspected Gus might even reconfigure some of her initial misconceptions from their blind-date debacle. Not that Cal wanted to date anyone right now, but she did find Gus attractive and likeable, and she hated to think her own inability to establish a favorable first impression might disappoint Em. This camaraderie they had going today was infinitely more favorable in her mind. She smiled at Gus and was pleased to see Gus smile back.

Dan Argyle walked in and dicked over her good mood like a dark cloud pissing on a parade. He inserted himself directly in front of Gus, invading her personal space with his creepy mustache and his customary *Mister Rogers' Neighborhood-ish* version of flirtation that just skirted the line between appropriate and inappropriate in the workplace. She could see the sweat glistening on the back of his emerging bald patch, and beyond him, Gus was actually smiling. Why would she even encourage this dorky schemer and his self-promoting power plays? Couldn't she see right through him just by the way he tucked his polo shirt into his track pants like a pedophile?

He said something just low enough for Cal to be unable to hear. Gus laughed and introduced herself, "I'm the new volunteer organizer for mental health services, supporting the inner San Antonio shelters."

69

Douche-bag Dan stepped to her side, titled his head toward Cal, and mimed a sickly sympathetic look at Gus. "Then I suppose you already know the sort of trouble you're traveling with." He wiggled both of his eyebrows up and down, and Cal couldn't believe that Gus giggled.

"Yes. I'm starting to realize just how awesome Andy and Cal are."

"I see. Well, I hope I can count on you to help me harness more of their enthusiasm toward recruiting some new corporate sponsors. They tend to get lazy and rely on companies owned by the Tylers and the Alexanas." He patted Gus's arm and Cal flinched for her.

"We've already recruited the two new sponsors you've required of each of us," Cal interjected.

Dan smirked. "As I said, those hardly count since they're already co-corporate sponsors of other projects with Tyler Groceries."

"I don't see why that matters," Andy came to the rescue, "It's often the same companies that care about similar charitable works and grow to trust their donations to efforts where their usual co-sponsors already donate. Help is help."

Gus nodded. "It never hurts to recruit extra and expand the network in new directions though."

"Exactly my point, Dr. Stuart. Thank you." Dan gloated a microsecond, before moving on to the front of the room.

Gus has no idea what kind of egotistical shenanigans she's fueling. Obviously, Gus knew better. She, herself, had zero tolerance for fakers like Dan Argyle, and she knew this hurricane season under his regional leadership was going to be rough.

†

70

"Okay, boys and girls don't forget that hurricane season lasts through November. Know when all of your designated shelter centers need to go into action and what services you need to coordinate where—before you need to know, if you know what I mean." Dan dismissed them with an upbeat reminder, despite having taken them through a meeting agenda with over eight hours' worth of information. Vain as the doughy man appeared to be, Gus had to credit his public speaking stamina.

She was exhausted just from listening, but she was still concerned about an insufficiency of mental health services available to displaced families at the inner-city Red Cross shelters in San Antonio, especially given any long-term displacements. As they were at the back of the room and it took Cal a while to gather her two laptops, smartphone, and assorted accessories, they were the last ones to leave. Gus decided she should at least start the conversation.

"I know you guys have a long-standing logistics plan for all the inner-city shelter locations, but I'm a little worried about providing mental health services with the few qualified volunteers we have at so many large and far-flung locations."

Cal's gaze was soft and understanding as she nodded at Gus. "Yeah, we've thought about that, too, and I think we have a workable solution, for this season at least." Her raspy, weary voice made Gus wonder if she would sound like that in a rumpled bed on a Sunday morning. The image warmed her chest and hands despite the over-air-conditioned room.

Cal cleared her throat before continuing, "I know the mental health services aspect was just added to Harbor House this year, and you don't have a lot of practitioners recruited to help out during disaster relief efforts, so I bargained with one of the corporate sponsors to get an empty facility in the middle of our shelter locations that we've dedicated for social work and mental health services. It's

71

near a normal bus stop along the river, and the city is willing to start running additional bus routes from each of the shelters, four or five days after a shelter opens until the shelter is closed again." Her glossy dark hair fell forward and covered her eyes, as she shouldered the black messenger bag now loaded with her electronics.

"Four or five days after each shelter opens could be seven to ten days after a family has experienced the complete loss of their home in a storm, or worse yet, the loss of a family member in a disaster."

Cal tossed her hair out of her face and gave Gus a blank, blue-eyed stare.

Gus rubbed her bottom lip and glanced at Andy. He stayed focused on his smartphone, texting someone. She felt like her point was about to prickle Cal the wrong way, and she wasn't sure why. "I appreciate your forethought and your work to organize something convenient to both families and mental health service volunteers, Cal. I know these kinds of programs are always subject to the whims of the regional boards that have to choose which of a multitude of needs are the priority."

"Good. Then you appreciate how difficult it was to get everyone to even consider mental health services as a necessary part of disaster response."

"I do, Cal. I promise, but that doesn't change my concern about it taking too long to get families access to those services after they've experienced a trauma."

Cal scratched her temple. "If you can recruit enough volunteers, then we could put one mental health practitioner at each shelter for the first few days. At least they could triage issues until the bus lines could run."

"The shelters will likely be too crowded and noisy to lend families and practitioners the space they need."

"Most of them, yes, but as you said yourself food, water, and shelter are the first priorities."

"That's not exactly what I said."

"Yes, I think it is." Cal crossed her arms and looked down her perfectly straight, aristocratic nose. Her blue eyes were becoming an icier shade of grey, like frozen water over a very deep winter pond.

"I know food, water, and shelter are of importance and certainly the focus of most disaster relief responses, but I don't think they are really as big a priority as anyone's will to live. Folks survive all kinds of disasters for days without food and shelter, so long as they have hope and confidence in their ability to survive."

Cal scoffed. "This isn't a third world country or an episode of *Survivor*."

"My point is, making people wait for several days to take a bus to stand in line at yet another overcrowded facility with yet another large group of strangers before they get help processing their grief and anxieties is asking for trouble. It could easily lead to disaster."

"Well, it hasn't yet, and that's good enough for me."

Gus's gut churned, as her anger flared up. "Texas has never before had twenty-five named storms predicted for a season, after already record flooding in Houston. Just because it hasn't been a problem before doesn't mean it will never be one. What happens when a million people suddenly need shelter after a Katrina type storm hits one of Texas's big cities? You've never experienced sheltering that many aggrieved families at once, as far as I can tell."

"No, we haven't, and we've also never had a mental health services coordinator before. We're already trying to prepare, but food and shelter take precedence."

"Over mental health?"

"Yes."

"No, they don't. I'm sorry, but you have to understand—"

Cal interrupted, "Go ahead, argue with me. It's not like I'm the only one you have to convince, for crying out loud."

"No, but you're—"

"Jesus, you're like a rat terrier," Cal interrupted again.

Gus sighed, she could feel Cal pushing her buttons, and she didn't want to lose her cool. She squeezed her hands into fists and let out a long, frustrated breath.

"I don't know why you're so wound up about this. Maybe it's like Andy says, and that means you really have the hots for me," Cal blurted.

"What?" Gus's voice twisted higher and louder, despite her best intentions. "As if." She crossed her arms and glared.

"Leave me outta this." Andy raised his hands and took a step away from them. "I definitely don't want my drunken generalizations remembered and recirculated."

Cal snorted and shook her head. "Look, what I mean is that I don't think I should have to explain to a psychologist the necessity of self-care, but somehow you don't seem to get it."

"I get it. You want us to take care of the bottom of Maslow's hierarchy of needs. You think they need food, water, shelter, etcetera, before we worry about caring for their emotional needs. But it doesn't work like that, Callia."

"No, that isn't what I mean. I mean you have to learn to walk before you can run. You have to take care of yourself, before you can take care of others."

"They'll get the basics first, regardless, that is already part of the plan. It's already a given that adding mental health service availability won't take away from."

Cal shook her head. "I'm talking about your care, our care, not theirs."

"That doesn't make any sense. We have food and shelter. We're already better off than the victims we're helping. The trickle-down theory of mental health care is a Republican fantasy."

"Now, don't go bringing politics into this. I just meant it would be best to plan for maintaining your own sanity, some, before you launch your mental health disaster service plan, because once you're responding to the disaster, you need to remember to do more than just eat and sleep. We have to be able to take care of ourselves, and be careful not to bite off too much too soon."

"Well, duh."

"Well, duh me all you like, but from what I've seen and heard of your work ethic, Dr. Stuart, you're a damn martyr to exhaustion."

"How would you know?"

"I have ears and eyes."

"Oh, yeah, well have you ever heard of projection?"

"Whatever. I'm not projecting my own flaws onto you, but you just use whatever flavor of denial suits you, honey."

Apparently, Andy felt a need to step in and get them on the road home. "Whoa, ladies, ladies, let's call a temporary truce, shall we? We still have to drive back, so can we bury the hatchet for now?"

†

When Andy pulled into Gus's drive it was dark. Before he could say anything, Cal bolted out of the back seat and opened the car door for Gus.

"Thank you for the ride, Andy. It was nice to meet you," Gus said, before she stepped out and walked past Cal toward her dark porch.

"You too," Andy called, as he watched Cal trail Gus to the edge of the porch. Neither woman said one word to the other, as far as he could make out, but Cal did wait until Gus entered the house and shut the front door again before she walked back to the car.

Cal folded herself into the passenger seat and shut the door. "Home, James."

"Hmm."

Cal looked over at him. "What?"

"You're acting a little weird, even for you."

"What do you mean?"

"You're happy and open one minute, and then the next you're as stiff and spiny as a new set of spurs. You can't stand her, but you can't take your eyes off her." Andy pointed toward the house with his chin and put the car in reverse, carefully backing the Prius over the pitted drive.

"What is weird is how freaking attractive she is…there is no reason for it. She isn't even the type of person I'm normally attracted to, or the kind of person I want to be attracted to." Cal let out a long breath and ran her hands through her hair, pulling one strand out over her left eyebrow as if to examine it more closely.

"What do you mean she isn't your type? Okay, so your track record doesn't exactly say that you appreciate dangerously hot, highly competent women with a higher social calling. Sure, based on your history, you're generally more into emotionally detached flakes…" Andy paused, realizing he probably didn't need to think entirely out loud. He came to a stoplight and glanced at Cal.

She glowered at him.

"Um, I mean, what I meant was…. Isn't Gus the kind of person you want to be attracted to? She's personable, tries to help people, isn't attracted to money or possessions, and at least on the hetero-male-hottie index, I'd say she's a ten outa ten. What don't you like exactly?" He was baffled by the contradictory hot and cold tones of their interactions. He knew they'd had one date gone bad, but he hadn't heard anything to suggest something really went wrong beyond a few awkward moments.

"Oh, where do I start to count the ways?" Cal held up her hand and raised a finger for each reason listed. "She's judgmental. She assumed from the start, before I opened my mouth, that I was a spoiled techie girl playing around. She's impractical about the realities of organizing disaster relief. She's so wrapped up in her own cause, she can't see the importance of making sure everyone is fed first, and she refuses to listen to reasons otherwise. She's a wannabe debutant who unconsciously flirts with Dan-the-dumb-dick Argyle, even after he's obviously an ass. She just drives me nuts, and yet she has apparently got my brother and my best friends convinced she's the cat's pajamas." Cal ran out of fingers, closed her hand into a fist, and hit the meaty edge of her hand onto her own thigh.

And there it was, jealousy, the real reason Gus overheated Cal into an inferno. Cal probably wanted Gus to think as well of her as Cal's friends and family already thought of Gus. "She wasn't flirting with Dan you numskull. That was just polite diffusion or some other sneaky shrink trick of killing the despot with kindness."

"Whatever." Cal sulked, and he knew he was right after all.

"She was, however, often flirting with you."

Cal gave him a sideways glare and bit her lip. "I doubt that, and it doesn't matter anyway."

Chapter Fourteen

I've Got a Kung Fu Heart.

It was after five o'clock, and Emily had already left. Gus was tidying up the waiting room when Andy walked in.

"Hey, Andy. It's good to see you. I'm afraid Emily already left." She greeted him with a smile.

He gave her a great big grin and shook his head softly. Even that gentle shake was enough to toss around the fine wisps of hair thinning over his forehead. "I actually came to steal you away."

"Oh?" Gus put down the parenting magazines she'd been arranging and turned her whole body toward him.

"Yeah, how do you feel about kung fu?"

Gus put one finger to the bottom of her lower lip, as she tried to decipher his meaning. "Kung fu is definitely a cool physical art form that I know absolutely nothing about." She crooked one eyebrow at him.

"Ah, I should have been more specific. How would you feel about going with Cal and I to see some really cheesy kung fu flicks at a historic theater called the Aztec?" Andy shifted his weight from one foot to the other and clasped his hands above his belt buckle.

"Sounds like it could be fun."

"The films are played in silence with subtitles, because a neoclassical instrumental ensemble called Two-Star Symphony is providing a live soundtrack. It seemed like something you might enjoy."

Gus nodded and glanced at the clock above the waiting room door, thinking that it wouldn't hurt to leave work and do something social at least one day of the week. It would prove to Callia Alexana that she wasn't all work and not enough play. She wondered if Callia really wanted to put up with her through the whole event though.

Andy cleared his throat. "Also, Nik catered the appetizers and his famous margaritas for the preshow happy hour."

Gus decided that it didn't matter what Callia wanted, she could make sure she had a good time getting to know Andy more, if nothing else. "I'd be delighted, Andy. It is very sweet of you to ask and to come by to pick me up."

Andy bounced on the balls of his feet and gave a smiling shrug, as he gazed toward the ground. "My pleasure, Gus."

"Just let me turn everything off and lock up back there, and I'll be ready to go."

"You bet."

†

Andy guided her into the lobby of the historic theater, and she was awed by its Mesoamerican splendor. Chicly dressed people glided smoothly over a rich, red and gold carpet, some of them merrily clustered around waitstaff with well-balanced trays full of multicolor, miniature martini glasses. Lively cello music drifted above them, and the acoustics were somehow great, despite the ornate plaster carvings covering every visible inch of wall. The music swelled, and Gus's eyes traveled up to the ceiling in front of the steps to the balcony level. The chandelier suspended from the center was a work of art, meticulously crafted from gilded steel and a rainbow of stained glass by someone who, surely, had either apprenticed under or adored the work of Louis Comfort Tiffany. Andy touched her elbow when the music abated. The crowd had diminished to reveal Callia Alexana. "Beautiful," she mumbled.

"I'm sorry. What was that?" Andy leaned in closer.

"The theater. It's beautiful," Gus replied, and she smiled without taking her eyes off Cal, who, despite everything, was even more beautiful than the theater. Her dark hair was glossy and burnished in the lobby's golden light. She wore navy sateen crop pants and a pale-blue suit vest under a navy blazer with the sleeves rucked up to her elbows. The lack of any shirt under the vest left visible swaths of olive-toned skin that made Gus's mouth go dry. Unlike their prior meetings, tonight Cal looked every bit the executive of some up and coming tech company.

"I thought you would appreciate it." Andy's reply interrupted her gawking. "Let's grab Cal and get some good seats. The theater itself is even more amazing. You'll want some time to look around before they turn down the lights for the films."

"Okay." Gus followed him across the room to Cal, but found herself still tongue-tied.

"I wasn't sure you would come," Cal greeted her. She held herself straight and tall, arms slightly askance.

Gus swallowed.

"What Cal means is that we weren't sure you were a kung fu fan." Andy stood to one side of the space between Cal and Gus.

Gus finally found her voice again. "It's beautiful here."

"Yes, it is, but I wasn't sure you'd appreciate the company." Cal put her hands in her pockets and leaned back on her heels.

Gus didn't miss the lightening quick flicker of hurt and uncertainty on her face. Her stomach clenched in response, and she found that her appetite for any of the hors d'oeuvres circulating the room completely evaporated. "I do. Thank you for thinking to include me."

"Oh, good." Cal's right hand slipped back out of her pocket, and she rubbed the back of her neck, looking more certain. "You're welcome. Want to go in?"

"Yes. Andy says it's even prettier in the theater." Gus was glad to see Cal's calm confidence restored. Her stomach unclenched, but her appetite was still long gone. Cal smiled, and butterflies replaced the earlier hint of hunger pangs.

"He's right. I think the small, center balcony is the best spot, but it can seem a little high." She tilted her head toward the stairs. "Are you game?"

"Lead the way."

Cal nodded and led them up the stairs, through a door, and down a dim aisle to a boxed set of four seats beneath an azure ceiling frescoed with gilded stars. She seated herself in the right most chair and gestured for Gus to take the small, red velour just beside her.

Gus looked to Andy, who nodded at her to go ahead. "I'll take the outer seat, and if no one sits in the fourth, then I can stretch my legs."

It made sense to Gus, as he was a tall guy. Putting her in the center probably made a lot of sense, because Cal was tall too. The seats were close. Even with her hands folded in her lap, she rubbed shoulders with both of them. Cal's felt warmer than Andy's. Gus cast her eyes around the theater, determined to marvel at the setting more than her company. Faux baroque columns and arches were outlined in an arresting mix of two-toned marble bands and limestone carvings of vaguely Aztec-looking geometric patterns. Backlighting made the azure ceiling look like the sky above a stone-walled garden. Bronze, wall sconces, shaped like torches, trailed delicate green leaves of glass, and gave off red-gold light. On stage, just to the side of the movie screen, sat three gilded chairs and music stands.

"The music is good. I know it seems weird to pair a cello ensemble with kung fu, but they're up to the challenge," Cal said. The pressure of her arm leaning closer covered more of the length of Gus's right arm.

"Which do you like more, the music or the kung fu films?"

"Well, I have to admit I have a kung fu heart, but in this case, the music is pretty damn good too."

The admission pulled a spontaneous laugh from Gus's belly. "I don't think I've ever heard anyone say it quite that way before." She smiled at Cal, and Cal gave her a crooked smile back.

The lights dimmed, the ensemble took the stage, and the film began. These were the kind of films with subtitles, so the replacing the soundtrack with live music was no loss from Gus's point of view. The cello and two violins began a quirky battle of staccato notes punctuated by the chimes of a dark marimba. The music created a tension of its own, a sound of pride and longing unresolved, as the film's plot unraveled toward the first fight. A lone protagonist stood like a slender southern pine, firm but flexible, rooted but yielding, against a host of fighters in short, dark robes and cotton pants.

Gus felt Andy shift over a seat, leaving a chair between them. No one had taken the fourth seat in their cluster. This gave her room to shift her own body away from Callia Alexana's warmth, to give them both a hint of space, but she didn't want to budge. As a moth to a flame, she couldn't resist the comfort. It occurred to Gus that Cal had room in her end seat to lean away if she wanted; and yet the sides of their arms were molded together so that she could feel Cal's breath lifting her arm whenever she stilled her own for a second. Why was this touch so much more intimate and alluring than any of the more direct pats some of her recent dates had bestowed on her?

She took a deep breath and caught the scent of Cal's ginger perfume. Her mind stilled, as her body responded to her undeniable attraction. Her pulse quickened, and heat traveled south over her skin. Not that she would act on it, but she at least gave herself permission to bask in the glow of sensation for the length of the show.

†

Intermission left Gus alone with Cal, as Andy excused himself to the line for the restrooms. Cal stood up, so Gus stood to let her pass by, but she just twisted her hips in place and flopped back into her seat. The platinum-cased smartphone appeared from one of her pockets, and her olive skin was rendered pale green in the device's back light. So much for civility thought Gus.

She rolled her head back and forth, stretching out her neck muscles, and then eased silently back into her own seat.

Callia glanced at her. "Don't you need to use the ladies room?"

"Not really."

"Oh. Me neither."

Gus refrained from pointing out that she could see that, but what escaped her mouth wasn't any more polite. "But you can't resist the chance to play with your gadget."

Cal frowned, still tapping at the screen. "I own my own business. Some things can't wait. I have a duty."

"I've heard that before."

"Well, it's true."

"Oh, sure, it's always true, but I think it's more a matter of perspective."

Cal turned off the phone and slipped it back into her jacket pocket, the one farthest from Gus. "Oh, really? How so?" Her ample lips were primly pressed into a straight line.

Gus knew she was probably overstepping, but she still couldn't stop herself. "You perceive the details in your e-mails are more important or relevant than what you can get from the people directly in front of you right now." This was one of her pet peeves. "When in reality, the face to face conversations you could be having in the lobby, with real people, could lead to better business resolutions and opportunities that are harder to negotiate electronically."

Cal's lips relaxed into a sigh. "Yeah, you're right. I can see that."

Shocked, Gus continued staring at her mouth.

"The truth is that I'm just tired of people for the day." Cal's crooked grin was self-deprecating. "I'm an introvert. I've done my duty of interacting in person. I've met my daily quota, you know?"

Gus nodded. She wanted to ask if she counted as one of those people Cal was tired of. She wanted to slink away, but she knew that was just a retaliatory emotional reaction born from the snub she perceived to her presence. She forced herself to wait.

"I'm sorry. I'm not that good with people."

"Do you want to be?"

Cal laughed. "Some days. Some people."

"But not today?"

"I'd settle for being okay with you." Cal licked her lips. "I don't want to upset you."

Gus sighed. "I'm fine. It's a beautiful place. The music is good, and the films are engrossing." She left off admitting the company was attractive, thinking the feeling probably wasn't mutual. Truth was, she thought, she didn't really consider herself in the beautiful Callia Alexana's league in any sense. Not in terms of looks, or social class, or economic status.

Cal touched her forearm briefly and quirked an eyebrow as she asked, "But it was a rough day for you too, huh?"

"It was fine."

"I have a feeling your days are always fine. Even the ultrashitty ones."

"I have a duty, too," Gus mumbled.

"I can imagine that you hear plenty of things that are hard to sleep with. I don't know how you do it."

The lights flashed, and a five-minute warning tone sounded to let them know intermission was ending soon.

Gus shrugged. "I'm not special. There are others who bare harder duties. I've seen many people quietly do their duty, to serve a country or save a life—there are so many good reasons, really."

"But the reasons don't defeat the posttraumatic stress." It was a whispered confession from Cal that Gus knew probably spoke to a deeper, darker reason why the techno-brat sitting next to her didn't necessarily want to be good with people. Complicated emotional baggage loomed over her trim shoulders.

"They do their duty anyway, knowing they probably won't live long enough to find out if anyone appreciates it, or worse yet, knowing that they'll probably live through it but never sleep soundly through another night. And kids are especially pressured. They perceive a duty to love their

85

messed-up parents way beyond all reason. I work to keep myself willing to hear all about it, because it is my duty to listen with empathy and help them make their peace with it. But that empathy, trying to heal others, costs all caregivers, too. It can build up into a tidal wave of secondhand posttraumatic stress if we don't take care of ourselves," Gus admitted.

The noise of people shuffling back into seats surrounded them.

"I bet," Callia whispered in her ear.

"I won't let that happen to me."

"I'm glad to hear that, but do you think we can always keep it from happening to ourselves?"

Gus realized that she didn't have a genuinely thoughtful answer to that. She glanced up at Callia. The deep, blue eyes gazing back at her showed concern and curiosity. Gus knew this woman had baggage. Something made her seem insightful and yet still so gruff and socially awkward. Gus wanted to ask, in fact. She found her stomach burned with the desire to know, but she wasn't sure she could easily turn back once she waded into that forest. She convinced herself that casual friendly encounters were safest for both of them.

Chapter Fifteen

Morning Mullings

"Do you think either one of them has a clue?" Nik asked his wife, as he stared at the ceiling above their bed.

Emily thought about it. She knew he was mulling over everything Andy had told them about Cal's behavior during their kung-fu-flick expedition with Gus last Thursday. She snuggled closer in where she was tucked up underneath Nik's arm, hugging his side, her head resting on his chest. She loved the way he smelled in the mornings, before his soapy smell of cedar smoke got lost amidst the forest of kitchen smells that permeated his daily domain. She sighed and let her cheek rest against the thin, soft, clean cotton of the undershirt he habitually wore to bed. "No, I don't think they have a clue. Do you have a clue how wonderful it is to be able to laze around in bed with you after the sun has risen?"

"Yes, I definitely have a clue how wonderful it is to be able to lay here cuddled up with you instead of arguing with the produce delivery guy after only one cup of coffee. But you know this is only so wonderful because it is such a rarity."

"Oh, I think I could have appreciated it even if it wasn't a rarity." Emily gave Nik's rib a slight tickle.

Nick laughed and squirmed away a fraction of an inch. "Hey now, no fair tweaking the sleepy bear, Goldilocks. Besides I'm trying to hold an intelligent conversation with you here. Why do you think that Callia and Gus are so hard on one another, when they are so obviously attracted to each other?"

Emily thought about it again. The sweet silence spread out like a baby blanket around them. A larger pool of sunlight inched its way across the floor with every minute. "I think that they're tripping over their preconceptions. Gus seems to think that Callia is entirely motivated by the need to play with flashy new technologies. She sees Cal as some sort of hard-as-nails entrepreneur, who is willing to walk over whomever or whatever obstacle gets in the way of the next big thing, just based on the simple fact that Cal is a successful businesswoman."

"Yeah," Nik agreed with Emily, "Callia says Gus is a petulant debutante, who is willing to champion any cause that is socially desirable, regardless of practicality or the social return on the charity. Yet, according to you and Andy, if you put the two of them in the same room they can't take their eyes off one another, and it isn't because they're giving each other the evil eye either."

Emily laid one small hand flat against the soft, sandpaper stubble of her beloved husband's square cheek. "It reminds me of seeing you or Callia in a room with Baba G'noush."

"Oh yeah?"

"It's like your surface and deep-level impressions of what Baba wants for you don't match, so your reactions to him span the gamut from hot to cold in the same season."

Nik cleared his throat. "So you think that Cal and I are tripping over our own preconceptions about Baba's motives?"

"Maybe," Emily answered.

A rumble passed through Nik's chest and into his belly. "Well let's start with me then. I think that Baba is never satisfied with anything we do, because it isn't the way that he would've done it. He does not approve of either of us, because we made career choices that he disagreed with. And even though he loves us, he holds a grudge about it. Which of those perceptions is potentially false?"

"I don't know. Maybe he is satisfied with some of the things that you do. Maybe he begrudges the fact that you pursued careers he disagreed with and they worked, but he is still proud of you. Or maybe it isn't disapproval at all. Maybe he questions every decision either of you make, because that is his nature. Baba is a natural devil's advocate. I think he thinks that he is being helpful by questioning every idea and helping to re-engineer and evolve it."

Nik remained silent.

Emily pressed on, "And maybe, the look that he gives you and Cal so frequently is really one of worry and hope for his two favorite rebels. Maybe, he thinks that you were never satisfied with him, or that you disagree with all of his advice, just because he did things differently than you would have liked."

Nik kissed the top of her head and squeezed her tighter. "Wow. I'm not sure that I am prepared to radically shift my perspective clear across the known universe like that before coffee."

Emily laughed and rubbed his belly before giving it a reassuring pat.

Several seconds passed in silence before Nik spoke again. "Thanks, Em." He took a deep breath and let it out slowly. "Let's go get a cup of coffee and sun on the plaza before it gets too hot. I promise, I'll think on it. Maybe, I can even get that bullheaded, Amazonian sister of mine to mull with me."

"I don't expect miracles, but I think she could only benefit from a little bee in her bonnet. She's definitely in a depressive rut. Any spark might be enough to jumpstart her on the road to happiness."

Chapter Sixteen

Unclaimed Baggage Is Even Worse

Gus worked to keep her expression open and neutral. She was beginning to suspect that something was rotten in Denmark. Farah Fowler had brought her seven-year-old son, Landon, in to see Gus, because despite Ms. Fowler's best efforts, the boy refused to speak much or interact with anyone on a meaningful level. His case wasn't unusual. Gus had seen dozens of kids in similar situations before, but this undersized seven-year-old boy was especially endearing. He was a stylized sort of beautiful that reminded Gus of one of the heroic drawings from the Manga books favored by some teenage girls.

Ms. Fowler had been a drug addict, and maybe she still was, but she was at least fit enough to convince the state to return Landon to her custody. She wasn't sure who Landon's father was, but the boyfriend who broke Landon's arm when he was two years old was definitively gone. Although, according to Ms. Fowler, her new steady beau did somewhat resemble the man who'd tossed Landon around before Child Protective Services temporarily removed him. Ms. Fowler was shaky, thin, and appeared twenty years older than she reported herself to be, leaving Gus to guess the drug dramas of the past were methamphetamine related; and there was no doubt that, even if she was recovered from her addictions, she still wasn't entirely recovered from the depression that plagued many people after withdrawal. Landon likely perceived that and it would only add to his anxiety that this new reality couldn't be entirely trusted. Or it could even be that Ms. Fowler really couldn't be trusted to care for him.

Landon did not make eye contact with Gus with his mom in the room. The one thing reassuring Gus was Ms. Fowler's immediate and hopeful consent when Gus had asked to be given some time alone with the boy. His mom was obviously, genuinely interested in just getting him to talk to someone, at least interested enough that she didn't worry about what he might say—or she was just that sure he wouldn't say anything. Gus wished she could be more sure, but Landon said little beyond answering yes or no questions and giving a guarded shrug when she asked him open-ended questions. He wasn't interested in playing anything or drawing or basically exhibiting any behaviors that might give Gus any insight into his state of mind. On the up side, he did make eye contact with Gus when his mom was out of the room, but that was breaking Gus's heart.

Their fifth session ended with the little guy, once again, curled up in a chair with his chin on his knees. His big eyes begged her to convince him she could be trusted. Gus would be patient. There wasn't much choice, but she worried that his circumstances might not favor them with enough time for him to become comfortable with her.

"Thank you for hanging out with me Landon. Would you like to go home with your mom now?"

He slowly nodded. A small twitch played down his left hand, and then he put his feet on the floor.

"You're free to go whenever you like."

He stood up, but didn't move any farther.
"Will you come back to see me again next week?"
He nodded more firmly this time.
"Great. I will be glad to see you."
He didn't smile, but something in his eyes looked a little less frightened. He scurried out of the room, closing the door behind him.

Gus sighed and remained cross-legged on the carpet, staring at the now empty chair a few feet in front of her. Optimus Prime, Batman, and a bobblehead Yoda complete with light saber lounged on a brightly colored set of Learning Resources Gears, incriminating her for Landon's lack of interest in them.

It was difficult for many children, especially troubled children, to articulate their problems, let alone the cause of their problems. Gus was forced to intuit a lot. With kids like Landon, she struggled not to assume too much. She knew it was important to give them a chance to explain or articulate their motivations on their own, but she wondered if some of them would ever be able to figure out what their motivations were. So many of the adults in their lives couldn't do it either. Parents like Farah Fowler frequently ended up lying about their motivations, either intentionally or unintentionally.

Gus considered herself staunchly nonjudgmental and accepting. Two parts of the mindset she thought were necessary to be good at helping kids. But was she losing some of that open-mindedness? She realized she was having a lot of trouble giving Farah Fowler the benefit of the doubt.

And then there was Callia Alexana. A woman who, by all accounts was a wonderful person, but Gus couldn't entirely trust that assessment. It was reasonable to be more critical in her personal relationships, right? Was it too much to want to be attracted to someone without an obvious clutter of emotional baggage? Someone with more social skills? She didn't think she could spare the energy or resources on complicated personal relationships. She needed her emotional reserves to keep the jadedness at bay, to be a good psychologist.

"And yet if you don't get a solid social life going soon, you'll start to feel isolated, and then you'll become too burned out to really help your patients." She repeated her sister, June's, warning to herself. She recognized that she needed a healthy life for herself before she could truly be good at helping others, but she was also afraid of getting distracted from work by someone who wasn't worthy. "It's good to be picky, right?" The imaginary June in her head just shrugged and looked doubtful.

Gus bit her lip and straightened her legs in front of her. She let out a large sigh and then whispered to the empty chair, "Am I kidding myself? Everyone has baggage, but if I've dealt with mine like I think I have, then why does my head still pound? Why can't I help Landon? Why am I still alone? Dear Lord, I know unclaimed baggage is even worse than lots of baggage. Please, give me the wisdom to see what baggage I haven't yet claimed."

Chapter Seventeen

Kindling Sticks

"What is she wearing?" Cal flicked her eyes over Emily's head and scowled toward Gus, indicating the clinician with a pointed glare.

"Since when do you care what anyone is wearing?" Emily asked.

"This is a tour of historic homes on a day that's going to easily hit a hundred degrees. Who is she trying to impress? And why is she here?" Cal protested, as she watched Gus smiling broadly at Huron and another board member, Hona Hayes. Gus's hands rose and fell painting a scene for her listeners. Huron kept his eyes on Gus's face, and his head tilted to one side. Hona had her whole body turned toward Gus and had one excessively diamond-studded hand placed at the corner of her mouth.

"Well, whatever Gus is wearing doesn't seem to be distracting the other guests. Whatever she is saying is keeping them engaged," Emily replied. "And I invited her, because I thought she would do a good job convincing perspective donors to donate. She's passionate about her work, and it's contagious when she tells others about it.

Besides, I did tell her this was a fundraising event and that there would be a tea in the garden before the trek. Maybe this is how people dress for fundraising garden parties in the deep south."

Cal stared at Gus again. Her wavy sienna hair hung loose and lustrous, as if she expected to shoot a hair-conditioning commercial. She wore hose, heels, and a vintage-looking, cap-sleeve dress of some silky, chocolate fabric with finely embroidered umber accents. Soft rucking that folded near her neck hinted that she had cleavage to spare without showing a damn thing, except a very conservative and small string of pale, freshwater pearls. She wore one very diminutive gold ring with a mother of pearl inlay in some design Cal couldn't make out at this distance, and earrings that dangled and glinted in the sunlight. She was the picture of a southern debutant and it made Cal's stomach ache. She didn't want to be here anyway, and avoiding her growing attraction to Gus on top of her other dreaded social obligations sounded especially exhausting.

Cal felt her stomach sink further, as Gus's honey-brown eyes noticed her and Emily under the oak tree. Her feet rooted to the spot against her will, and her pulse quickened. She scowled a little more.

†

Gus finished talking to Huron and Mrs. Hayes, and scanned the crowd to find Emily. She thought talking to Emily might still her nerves. No one was dressed up as much as she was. She hadn't known what to expect, and her mother liked to remind her that it was better to be overdressed than underdressed. She wondered if someone had passed out a memo telling everyone else to show up in linens, tennis whites, and sandals. She was too hot, even in the shade. She would have to go back to the bigger crowd in the air-conditioned sun porch. As she contemplated a path over the courtyard stones, her eyes traveled over the big old oak and its impossible greenness. Under the shading limbs, Emily rested with her back to a low branch, and beside her, Callia Alexana's storm-blue eyes threw out enough sparks to light wet mulch. Gus's stomach clenched, and her mouth went dry. She forced a smile anyway and approached the pair.

Callia towered over Emily, extra tall, lithe and dark in contrast to Emily's dainty blonde curves. Emily had on a simple and trendy version of the ubiquitous linen shift, a couple of silver bangles, and a pair of Huaracha sandals. Her perfectly straight and thick, blonde hair was pulled into a neat ponytail and fastened with a bit of leather cord wrapped nicely at the base of her neck. Callia maintained her techno-brat look, but still somehow fit into the scene in a flowing pair of natural-colored linen pants and a pale-grey, boat-necked tunic; the shoulders cut artfully away, creating a dramatic edge against the perfectly buff roundness of her shoulder muscles. *Even Madonna, famous for her well-muscled arms on stage, would still kill for arms like that,* thought Gus. There was no denying Callia was attractive. She even made her pair of reef flip-flops somehow look like the natural fashion choice of the day. *Curses on all the tall, beautiful, and exotic looking corporate heiresses.*

"Hello," Gus managed to eke out, as Callia kept up the intense eye contact with her. "I didn't know you would be here too." Gus couldn't help but smile a bit. It was a reflex she always tried with glowerers. Research showed that it was harder for someone to yell at you or stay set against you if you were smiling at them. Even if they did yell at you, they were left irked and wondering why you kept smiling at them. It did seem to startle Callia.

Cal backed up a step, retreating from the hot, brown-eyed gaze that seemed to be sucking up all the oxygen nearby. She found herself stuck in place by the wide oak branch behind her.

"My home is on the tour," Callia said, as she watched Gus's face. Gus had on a light dusting of makeup, a faint trace of pink lip gloss. Callia felt herself blush. Why was she looking at Gus's lips anyway?

"Oh, really? You live out here in Alamo Heights then?" Gus replied. "I'm surprised you don't live in one of the hipster, overpriced lofts above some art gallery, closer to the roaming packs of city nightlife."

"I like the quiet."

"You like the quiet? So you and every neighbor in a five mile radius can fully appreciate the jet-decibel sound of your monster motorcycle?"

Cal snorted. It figured the debutant would have a snide remark about her mode of transportation. "Ah so, saving children from the mental anguish they were born into is important, but minimizing your carbon footprint doesn't take priority over appearances?"

Gus's mouth opened a bit into a rounder shape, and then smoothed into a demur smile. "I'm sorry, Callia. I think I just insulted you for riding a motorcycle, didn't I? I'm not sure why I'm so judgmental-sounding right now."

Cal licked her lips and crossed her arms. She wanted to grab the pesky shrink and shake some pretensions out of her...*and kiss her too*, added a small voice in the back of Cal's head. *Ah hell*, thought Cal, *who asked you, libido*? She consciously dropped her crossed arms. "I guess that comment about your carbon footprint was a bit ridiculous, since you don't even own a car."

"A little bit," Gus admitted, "but given how little the bus lines are used here, you could probably argue that my individual portion of the bus's carbon emissions are probably still larger than your motorcycle's."

Cal's mind stubbed its toe on the proverbial incongruity in their last few words. Gus would be devastatingly attractive in an all-American way if she reserved her bitter judgments like this all the time. But then again, it probably didn't matter, because she wasn't really ready to be attracted to anyone in her current funk.

Sensing it would be stupid to hope for more progress than these two muttonheads had already achieved with their first congenial conversation of the day, Emily interrupted, "Well then, it is settled."

Gus and Cal both glanced at Emily, as if noticing she was still there for the first time in several minutes. The blank-goldfish, short-memory looks they were giving her did not go unnoticed. She clapped her hands as she would for a small gathering of kindergartners and gave directions, "Now, don't you two think it's time we got this tour of the renovated, historic homes of Alamo Heights started?"

Emily did not wait for a response but turned and strode toward the all-glass sun porch, where the majority of guests waited. She watched Cal and Gus reflected in the glass as they followed her inside, a few steps behind, each in her own world but somehow still looking like part of the same team.

Chapter Eighteen

Hot Flash

Gus had not planned on participating in the tour, but curiosity got the better of her once she learned that she'd get to see Callia's house. She had played this game with herself since childhood. She would try to predict what her schoolmates' homes must look like, based on the way her schoolmates behaved, what they wore to school, and how they talked about their families. She'd secretly revel any time she got a chance to actually see what a schoolmate's home was really like and hence check her imagination's predictions against reality. Being a psychologist, having the required occupational curiosity about human behavior, came naturally to Gus. She was eager to find out if Callia would occupy the sleekly modern, posh minimalist abode she supposed to be the techno-brat's most comfortable domain. She suspected Callia had hired an industrial architect, and that most of the renovations involved lots of straight lines, open spaces, and steel and glass. Gus was also delighted to learn that the Tyler family home would also be included. She set about imagining rolling green expanses, plantation columns, and trellises as a possible home for Texas's most successful grocery distribution magnate and his heirs. Of course, Gus had to admit that she based this prediction entirely on her one experience visiting an uber-wealthy, TV executive's home in Atlanta. This was not Gus's social circle. Her only exposure to wealthy society had been through the few parties given by the dean at her graduate school. The dean was married to some rockstar neurosurgeon, and his salary was just extra money on top of his wife's earnings. Gus recognized that her meager experience with the expression of American wealth and high society, coupled with her Peace Corp days, likely skewed her expectations, severely.

As they walked up the long drive of the second house on the tour, Gus saw Nik walking out the front door. As far as she could tell, Nik had only one set of interchangeable clothes consisting of black chef pants, white chef top with sleeves always rolled above his elbow, and a pair of black, chef clogs. He and Callia were obviously family, sharing similarly beautiful olive skin tones and piercing blue-grey eyes. Only, Nik smiled a lot more and seemed to shun all technical gadgets. She noticed Nik was scowling now, and the expression made him look like Callia's fraternal twin rather than her younger brother.

Gus watched, as Emily called out to him. He looked up as if surprised to see her, but the agitated twitching at the corner of his lip was replaced by a large smile. Emily beamed back at him, and they exchanged a few words Gus couldn't hear from her place near the back of the group as it paused. Nik quickly placed a kiss on the top of Emily's head and stepped toward the back of the group to get out of the way, as Emily continued to lead them toward the house.

Gus saw his face change, as she walked by him and he noticed her. He gave her arm a squeeze in greeting, effectively pausing her pursuit of the tour group. Nik and Emily both liked to chat. Maybe she could find out what had him scowling a minute ago. "Hey, Nik. I thought you'd be at work."

"Hi, Gus. I was, but it's slow on Sunday afternoon in the summers, so I thought I'd stop by and see the folks," he gestured with his thumb over his shoulder. "And find out how Em's tour was going."

"This is your parent's place?" Gus gestured with her chin at the turn-of-the-century, mission architecture and courtyard pockets that sprawled around them.

"Yeah. My great-great-grandfather built it in 1875, after his first Baba Alexana's deli really took off downtown. He wanted a place for the whole family to live in peace. A place with real walls, like the wealthy Texans had." Nik smiled proudly.

"Wait, you mean your family is the famous Alexana family?" Gus was astounded. She thought Callia and Nik's last name was just a coincidence, or that maybe they were distantly related to the giant restaurateur clan; but this meant that Nik and Callia came from an old line of plenty of money, as much or more so than Huron and Emily even. Gus suddenly felt herself swimming in a social circle she wasn't prepared to float in. These people had ridiculous amounts of money.

"Yeah. But that's mostly my dad's bag. He is Mr. Capital." Nik suddenly looked dejected.

Gus couldn't help herself, sometimes the psychologist just slipped out like an obnoxious possession by Freud. "Why does that upset you, Nik?"

Nik gave her a sad little smile. "I don't want my success to come from my family's history or my dad's connections. I want it to be that I came up with a good idea and worked my ass off to make it work. And I want people to say there goes Nik Alexana, the chef that changed restaurants—not there goes the guy that expanded his family's restaurant empire."

"Well, at least you are trying on your own, and it will be obvious whatever wealth and success you accumulate is all your own—I mean it isn't like you used your family's money and connections to buy your house or start your business. Like Cal did."

Nik twitched and gave her a look of pure incredulity. "Callia? She didn't take a dime from our parents. She refused to even let them pay for her education. She created her first programs all on her own and got the financing from the bank to build her business."

His revelation smacked Gus mute.

Nik wrung his hands and then shrugged. "She makes it even harder for me to measure up in my own mind, I guess, because I know she did it all on her own. She has out-earned Baba's projections without a bit of advice from him. I have to waddle over and ask his advice to even have a clue how to manage my capital assets well enough to consider supporting a second cafe…and then I don't even have the decency to like what he tells me, when I know it's sound advice."

"Oh." Gus was still caught up thinking of Cal paying her own way through school.

"Why are you so hard on her?" Nik asked, one eyebrow quirked, evoking that eerie similarity between him and Callia again.

"I'm not hard on her," Gus protested.

"Come on, Gus, really? You assume I'm all self-made but she isn't? I've seen you give me, Emily, and Huron the benefit of the doubt, even when we're probably being a bit snobby, but from what I hear, you're quick to scold Cal for less."

"I don't know, Nik. I just hold her to higher standards, I guess. Maybe because I met her in a dating context first." Gus rubbed the back of her hot neck and lifted her thick hair off her overheated skin for a second.

103

"I don't get it. From what I know and everything that Em says, it isn't like you to be so judgmental. I've never even heard of you making a judgmental comment about one of the patients, whom I know Emily believes are certified low lifes."

"That's different. I'm supposed to err on the side of unconditional acceptance with them. Callia isn't a patient."

"Okay, I get that. But you still don't make such harsh, presumptive judgments about Em or me, or even about Huron's tomcat, slutbag, bimbo-izing."

"You're my friends."

"So Callia isn't your friend?"

"No, she's not my friend, she's—"

Nik interrupted, "Now wait a minute, my sister is a damn good friend to have on your side, and she certainly doesn't have a thing against you."

"That isn't what I meant, Nik." Gus held up both hands, afraid she'd hurt him.

"Then what? I don't understand. So what if the date didn't work? Why isn't she your friend?"

Gus sighed and noticed her hands trembled a bit. "I don't know. She's still a date to me, I guess. It didn't work, but I still think of her that way, for some reason, and I hold those I date to a higher standard than I do my friends."

"Oh Gus, those must be impossible standards if my sister can't meet them, or you're not giving her a fair shot at them."

Gus had a moment of doubt, but she covered over it with the counter argument bristling in her subconscious. "It doesn't matter. She doesn't like me either."

"Hmm," Nik capitulated. "Well you do seem to set off her temper in some weird way, but who's to say that isn't unrequited attraction chapping her hide?"

Gus stared over his shoulder, noticing the tour group was long gone.

Nik turned his head, following her gaze. "I guess I've kept you from the tour, huh?"

She shrugged one shoulder, unsure if she should continue the tour anyway.

He extended his hand to her. "Come with me? I'll escort you in and catch you up."

She took his peace offering for what it was and accepted his hand.

He guided her up the drive way and through the massive front doors of studded oak.

†

"Nikolai, you're back." A bespectacled man with mousy brown hair greeted them in the foyer. "And who is this with you?"

"Baba this is Dr. Augusta Stuart, the supervising clinician from Harbor House's mental health services clinic." Nik touched her shoulder. "Gus, this is my dad, Simon Alexana."

A willowy woman, who wore her age very well, glided into the foyer with a vibrant smile and held hands with Mr. Alexana. "And I am Nik's mother. Please call me Lorina."

"Thank you. Please call me Gus. You have a beautiful home."

Nik laughed. "Humble as it may be."

"We're very blessed," Lorina replied, as she turned her radiant smile toward her son.

Nik returned her smile and nodded. "Mamma, I promised that I would help Gus catch up to the tour. Are they still here?"

"They are. I'm happy to escort you through, Gus."

Nik asked, "Is that okay, Gus? I should get back to the café before dinner service starts."

Being left alone with the Alexana matriarch was daunting, but Gus couldn't bring herself to ask Nik to stay and run interference. She nodded. "I appreciate it. I don't mean to impose."

"There is no imposition." Lorina's eyes were the same striking shade of darker, blue-grey as Nik and Callia's.

Mr. Alexana asked, "Are you sure that you can't stay, Nikolai? Someone else can run the dinner service. We would love to have more time to spend with you."

Nik sighed and stuck his chin out. "I'm sure, Baba. I will see you for coffee tomorrow morning." He blew a kiss to his mother and left in a hurry.

"Please excuse my children, Dr. Stuart. They seldom find time for what is most important." Mr. Alexana pushed his spectacles up his nose with his fore finger and smiled sadly at Gus.

"They work hard," she offered.

"Not always a plus." He shook his head, and the light hit the fine grey hairs at his temple. "They do not need to work so hard. We have plenty of blessings already that they fail to fully enjoy, and they deprive the rest of us of the joy of sharing time with them."

"I'm sure you are proud of them though. They couldn't work so hard without the love and support of good parents," Gus answered.

"I would rather they let me love and support them more. I have been around the block already, so to speak."

Lorina let go of his hand and turned her beautiful gaze to him. "I believe they want to show us how well they can do on their own sometimes. Now, enough of your sadness for today. I'm going to keep my promise and help Gus catch up to Emily."

106

Mr. Alexana laughed. "Yes, my love. It has been a pleasure to meet you, Dr. Stuart. I can see why Emily speaks so highly of you."

Gus felt herself blush. He shuffled away before she thought of a reasonable reply in kind.

"Shall we?" Lorina invited her along.

†

Lorina took Gus through the parts of the house that Emily had already toured. Consequently, they barely caught up with Emily as the group was leaving the Alexana's home. Lorina quietly bid Gus good-bye with a wave and a wink.

As she followed the group down the winding drive and up the long side of the block, she continued to picture smaller versions of Nik and Callia in their sprawling adobe, childhood home. She coveted the rainy days they must have spent playing with toys on the mix of Turkish and Navajo rugs in the library with the slung-back reading chairs of raw cowhide. The square, mission-style wood furniture smelled of linseed oil and brass polish, and exhibited smoother patches on the top surfaces where Gus pictured generations of Alexana's reading. As a child, she would have chosen to hide there, and she found herself wondering if Nik and Callia had. In many of the family pictures, their older, blonder brothers—Hans and Coen were the names Gus remembered from her blind date with Callia—stood patiently behind Nik and Cal, wearing expressions of tolerant affection for the younger, darker Alexanas. The age gap appeared significant, and Hans and Coen didn't seem to figure prominently in Nik or Callia's daily lives. Lorina had explained they were both married with several children of their own already consuming their attentions. Gus could plainly see that Lorina was a woman who loved her children and her grandchildren.

The Alexana home seemed happy, and yet there was a detectable tension too.

The group turned the corner and proceeded on for two more blocks. The yards grew smaller and the houses more modest. Finally, they stopped before a simple, Craftsman-style bungalow. The low-pitched, gabled roof and broad eaves extended over a large front porch and exposed oak beams. Limestone covered the lower third, and pleasantly weathered cedar siding spread from there up to the roof. It was a beautiful bungalow with a carefully xeriscaped yard. Texas sage, blue aloe, flowering senna, and red yucca were alternated with artful beds of gravel and pale, granite stepping stones.

She could barely hear Emily talking at the front of the group, giving the history of the house, but she heard enough to decipher Callia's name. She would not have picked this understated house as Callia's in a million years. The fixtures were galvanized steel, and there was no evidence of advanced technology of any sort. The plain, solid oak door, of observably good quality, was definitely not new. Emily guided them in, where an old, varnished-pine floor was punctuated by plain brown rugs of some soft weave that Gus did not recognize. The walls were a pale parchment color, and there wasn't an electrical panel or speaker system affixed to any of them as far as Gus could see. Most of the furniture appeared to be restored pieces of vague, but not likely expensive, antiqueness. Except for a very pretty art deco, tigerwood buffet and dining table set just off the farmhouse-styled kitchen.

There were only two bedrooms. Both featured white iron bed frames and sparse, dark dressers with old, white marble tops, against chocolate walls. The bedding of one room was a varying mix of yellows, while the one Gus pegged as Callia's was a mix of blues. Milk bottles held dried sprigs of blue lavender and tall, dried ironweed on the dresser, and there was a walk-in closet attached to the blue-quilted room. She wondered, uncharitably perhaps, if the closet was where Callia hid all her high-tech toys and conveniences at home.

There was no sign of Callia, until they traipsed through the shady backyard toward the carriage-style garage tucked under a large live oak tree. Emily introduced her to the crowd and someone asked if they could see inside the garage. Callia obliged by opening one side of the sweeping barn doors facing her graveled driveway.

The man who'd asked about seeing the garage complemented Callia's motorcycle. Cal's eyes found Gus's gaze, and she replied to the earnest man, "Thank you. Not everyone appreciates the concept of motorcycles."

"Yeah, I hear you. My wife would never approve, or even give the idea a chance, I'm sure."

Cal smiled and flicked her gaze between the man and Gus. "Well, at least she's already married to you, so she isn't as likely to make a snap judgment about you because you're interested in them."

†

Cal watched as the crowd trailed away after Emily. She noticed Gus lingered behind. The psychologist looked like she wanted to say something, but she remained standing and silently looking toward Cal's motorcycle. Cal stepped back into the shade of the garage's eve, realizing too late that it brought her very close to where Gus was still standing. *Probably too close for common social comfort*, she admitted to herself. They were only inches apart, but she didn't move. She figured Gus could back off and follow the crowd away any time she wanted. But she didn't.

Cal could see the pulse in the hollow of Gus's throat; she wanted to graze her teeth and lips against it. She wanted to run her lips over the curve of Gus's pert jaw. She wanted to touch the smooth, compact muscles and bare skin of Gus's biceps to see if they really were like touching warm silk as she imagined. She wanted to kiss the delicate laugh lines just hinting at their full mirth in the corner of Gus's eyes, and her tiny elfin chin and impish nose. Her whole face spelled kindness. *Toward everyone else*, Callia's snarky mind added.

But Gus did smile up at her, and her eyes expanded and contracted in flashes of opulent gold and earth-dark brown like a tigereye polished and cut to show. Callia's snarky mind shut up, as something akin to a hot flash hit her.

Gus drew a deep breath. "You're right. I did make a snap judgment about you because of your motorcycle, and I haven't given the idea of motorcycles any real chance. Will you accept my apology?"

"Accepted." Cal nodded.

"Would you please show me?" Gus asked and gestured toward the garage door.

"Show you?" Cal rubbed the callous on the inside of her right hand where the slight pucker in the bike's grip usually rubbed.

"Yes, please. Show me, or tell me, or help me understand why you relish motorcycling. I don't understand the appeal or the advantages over the bus in this Texas heat and traffic."

"Okay." She ushered Gus closer toward the bike and pulled the barn door closed behind them. Sensing the relative darkness and their motion, the overhead lights came on. The bike's Arctic-white paint shined sleekly. The bright LED bulbs revealed the bike's stylistic lines to greater effect than the dusty sunlight had. Cal placed a bare hand on the cool gas tank. "Okay. Sit on it," she invited Gus.

"Um. I don't think that is a good idea. I don't know the first thing about how to get on one of those." Gus wrung her hands, but offered a timid smile.

"Okay. I'll help, and when you're comfortable, I'll explain the pros and cons as I see them." Cal believed in demonstrating things before talking specifications, a habit from her software engineering experience that seemed to have migrated its way into other facets of her life.

Gus remained rooted in place. "I don't want to sound like a stupid southern belle, but I don't want to swing an awkward leg over and bring the machine crashing to the ground in a snarl, with my soft parts competing with its heavy metal bits for the top spot."

Callia smiled a little. "I will help make sure that doesn't happen, if you would like," she offered.

"Yes, please," Gus said.

Cal swung one linen-clad leg over the bike and balanced herself on the very back edge of the bike's seat. She was tall enough, and strong enough to balance the café racer between her legs if needed. Gus was probably strong enough on her own, but wearing those all-too-impractical heels and hose with a dress made it more challenging. It made sense that she might have a hard time balancing the motorcycle without some support. Cal held out a hand, offering to help Gus settle on the seat in front of her.

Gus audibly swallowed and then took Cal's hand.

The fine cotton and silk blend of Gus's dress brushed against Callia's pants as Gus stepped one leg a little higher than needed over the lowest part of the bike's seat. Her dress bunched up a little higher on her thighs, revealing tantalizingly trim lower quadriceps. She could not keep both feet on the ground, even with the extra height her heels offered, and started to wiggle over to the top-heavy side of the kickstand. Cal quickly grabbed Gus's hips to steady her in place. "Easy there. Don't shift around so much, just let me balance the bike and you sit centered. Neither foot has to touch the ground. See those metal pegs just behind your heels?"

"Hmm," Gus murmured and felt back for the pegs until her feet connected. As she settled in, Cal kept her hands on the smaller woman's hips. Warmth spread up her sides and then her skin suddenly chilled when Gus grasped her upper thigh.

Cal struggled to keep her breathing even. She could smell Gus's shampoo, something fruity and sweet. "Ah, you can put both your hands on the handlebars there. Don't worry, I will help keep the motorcycle balanced upright."

Gus nodded and moved her hands to the handlebars.

The skin under Cal's pants flushed, and she missed Gus's warm grip on her legs instantly. "Okay, now let me explain the first attraction here."

Gus coughed and sputtered, "What? What do you mean?"

"The first attraction to driving this motorcycle around town," Cal answered.

"Oh. Right. Yeah."

"Are you comfortable?"

Gus wiggled, adding a little friction where her back touched Cal's breasts. Cal repeated the word *focus* in her head five times.

"Yeah, this is pretty comfortable," Gus admitted.

Cal cleared her throat. "Well, like I said then, the first attraction is that it is so comfortable. I put a lot of time into designing and building it so that there would be no wasted detail."

"How so?"

"Well, I'm not sure if you noticed, but it's a pretty bike."

"Yes, I did notice that part. It's like a sculpture."

"Yeah, that's a pretty good description. I've never thought about it like that, but it is like a sculpture. And yet everything on the bike is necessary for it to function. Every pretty part has a purpose."

"There is no bling," Gus admitted.

"Exactly, there are no badges, no stickers, no extra chrome detailing. Nothing extraneous, but it is still pretty and comfortable."

"That's how you define well made, then?"

"Yeah, and yet affordable. It's a third of the price of most Harley Davidsons, almost two hundred pounds lighter, too, and gets almost twice the gas mileage."

"It isn't fast, huh?"

"Oh, it is fast. Because it is so light, it accelerates faster than most bikes."

"The thrill is your second attraction to it?" Gus let go of the handlebar, and twisted her head enough to meet Callia's eyes.

Cal felt a thrill, but it wasn't from the thought of riding her bike. "Um, probably more like the fourth or fifth attraction."

Gus's brown eyes sparkled. "What's second?"

Cal smiled. "Parking and ecology. I can always find a spot to park, even in the most congested parts of town at the worst times. And I'm only one person, so I don't have to waste a lot of fuel pushing a truck around town just to drive myself to work."

"Oh." Gus's brows creased. "I didn't really expect those to be important to you."

"No? Well, I'm nothing if not practical. It's the logistics professional in me." Cal expected Gus's mask of disapproval to slip back in to place at any moment.

Gus's face remained open though. "Also very environmentally considerate of you."

113

Cal nodded. "I'm no saint, but I try."

"That's the best any of us can do." Gus patted Cal's thigh with one small hand. "Thank you."

"You're welcome." Cal kept the motorcycle anchored, as Gus slid her leg over and stood up. "How are you going to get home tonight?"

Gus smiled. "The bus. It leaves the stop, four blocks over, in—" Gus glanced at her bracelet watch— "Oh, shit, fifteen minutes."

Cal stood up and stepped toward her. "Well, if you like, I could give you a ride home. I've got another helmet and everything."

Gus's lips moved but no sound came out. Her head tilted.

Gus couldn't swear who started it, but there was a kiss. Two sets of lips met and sparks flew. No kiss had ever been as sweet as this one, this one that she didn't want to want so much. She stepped into the kiss. She didn't do it intentionally, her body just willed it, and there she was with her lips mapping the modelesque angles of Callia's wide mouth.

She felt the bubble of want burst in her throat and slide all the way down to her toes. She wrapped one hand in Cal's luxuriously soft, black hair and the other around Cal herself, bringing them entirely too close together for safety. She felt like she was drowning, and she clung to Cal like a lobster in a pot wanting to use the other lobsters as a step out of the fire. Gus couldn't contain the groan of want that escaped her belly and vibrated out of her vocal chords into the thinning air around them.

Cal's tongue brushed hers. A taste of sunshine. A wildfire of sensation swept clean the dense undergrowth of all her anxieties for one startling moment, before the smoky shrouds of doubt choked out the growth of her happiness again.

They both knew this had to stop. At least, Gus thought they must. She knew Cal didn't really like her, and she wouldn't throw herself at someone who didn't like her just because there was this unbelievable physical chemistry sparking between them.

She forced herself to pull back. "I, uh, gotta go." She turned on her heel and bolted out the barn door for the bus stop without giving Callia a backwards glance. She knew if she hesitated, if she met those intense eyes again, she would lose all will to resist that physical spark. Her id would rule her ego, no matter how preachy her superego got, and there she would be, falling in love with a woman who had a whole lot of complicated baggage. She just didn't trust that someone with so much baggage could really be a good partner for her. Ultimately, her exhausted empathy would leave them both burned out.

Chapter Nineteen

Warm Intentions

Huron paced in front of the large windows overlooking the adobe courtyard and gardens below. Simon Alexana had done well for his family, amplifying the empire he'd inherited from his ancestors. A corporation of national deli franchises was now a multinational, multirestaurant conglomerate. Huron was too young to know anything about Baba's youth, but he'd seen pictures of the bookish Simon when the older man was still the mousy "Baba Ghanoush" at his own father's knee. Simon had grown up and managed things, manipulated luck and fate to secure a business legacy. Proportionately, averaged across the years of their careers, Simon had made more money from less than Huron had, and Callia had done at least as well if you factored in the fewer years she used to earn it. Huron loved this family, who already included his family as part of theirs. There wasn't anyone who suited him as well as Callia. How could anyone else? He sighed and let his hands rest on the solid oak credenza beneath the window.

Callia claimed she was gay, but as far as he knew, her dating history didn't really authenticate that very well. There was no woman she seemed to take seriously enough to bring home at any rate. He stopped in front of the window and fumed, as he surveyed the yard below.

He was her equal. She was his equal. They were meant to be together. It didn't matter if she was a lesbian. She could always satisfy that urge on the fly with a willing mistress, if it persisted, as could he. What she needed for a spouse was an equal partner and the equal part was more important than the gender.

He just had to work hard enough, manipulate things right, and he would earn her over to his way of seeing it. Everything worth having had to be earned, and people seemed to forget that. Sometimes you had to earn things three or four times over, and most people gave up when they thought they'd done enough—just when it became apparent they needed to do more than enough.

Huron thought this was really at the core of what ailed most of society. Politicians wanted to distribute things no one had earned, so that the politician would be re-elected to an office they felt they'd done enough to earn but probably hadn't. One good deed, one good project, didn't get you anything for life. You had to keep re-earning it. He'd earned Callia's lifetime friendship, and he kept re-earning it. He'd earn her love too. He just need to make her jealous, and sabotage any potential competitors before they could break through Callia's gruff barriers. There was definitely some promising tension between Callia and Emily's latest find, Augusta Stuart. Worse yet, Lorina and Simon genuinely seemed to like Gus. Everyone did.

Huron thought it best if he kept to himself the nature of his interest in Dr. Stuart. Gus was a beautiful woman. Certainly, many men would consider her the perfect trophy wife, or even the perfect partner. That was reason enough for them all to believe Huron would be, could be, interested in

117

Gus. Huron pursuing her was credible. He could pursue Gus in such a way that it would look as if Gus pursued him, and he reasoned that would either cause Callia to dismiss Gus as fickle or out of jealousy. If Callia became jealous of the attention Huron gave Gus, all the better. Callia would come to Huron's rescue, she always did. Not that time with Gus would be painful. The woman was a looker. Huron's thoughts were interrupted, as Simon entered the study.

"I'm sorry to keep you waiting, Huron. How are things?" Simon asked, as he took a seat in the leather wingback chair closest to Huron and the window.

"Things are well, Baba Simon. I am well. I've just been thinking about Callia." Huron paused to gather his words.

"You're a good friend to my restless daughter."

"I hope to be. You know I've always wanted to be more."

"Yes, I do. I would love that as well, but you know that she thinks she is a lesbian."

"So she says."

Baba nodded and steepled his fingers. "It is a pity she doesn't seem attracted to you beyond your stellar friendship."

Huron nodded and put on a pained expression. Baba never drank, but Huron wished he did. He would have liked having their chats even more over a smooth, old scotch or an ice cold Mexican beer.

Simon rested his arms on the armrests. "You two make a strikingly smart and handsome couple. And I have no doubts that, together, you could give me even more amazing grandchildren to add to my precious passel."

He had to chuckle at that. "Yes, I would have loved to try."

"Hmm." Simon gestured for him to sit. "So you're giving up?"

Huron sat. "I think it may be time. Or at least time to try a different tactic."

"You know, when I met Lorina, she didn't see me as anything more than a friend. She was always sweet to me—the geeky, gangling boy I was then—but she really seemed to notice me when we were in our accounting class at UT together. I still don't know if it was because I was the only other one, of hundreds in that class, who seemed to enjoy accounting as much as she did—it was a number puzzle and the whole world went quiet when our minds were engaged in the world of accounting—or if it was just that I was familiar, polite, and adored the stunning Lorina Foch without threatening her independence. Something attracted her to me, and either way, I recognized true love when I saw it and did my best to nurture the spark we shared."

"I know, Baba. Forty years later you are still together, and I know you wish exactly that for all of your children."

"I do."

"I know you are not happy that Callia prefers women." Huron stared at his shoes. He knew he certainly wasn't happy about it.

"Actually, I don't so much care that Callia prefers women. I just wish she would settle down with a good one, and make me some grandbabies. So far, she has accomplished everything else in the damn world, except anything that would establish her as this family's matriarch. I wish she would have some children for us to enjoy before I'm too old to be of much use, and Lorina would like to know her only daughter is happy."

Too surprised by Simon's admission, Huron spoke more openly and less logically than he intended. "As far as I can tell, either Callia isn't attracted to sane women, or sane lesbians are such a rarity that Callia hasn't yet encountered an attractive one."

119

Simon laughed. "Maybe, but Nikolai hinted that the pretty little Dr. Stuart, with her sweet manners, likes Callia. Although I can't say that Callia has specifically mentioned any particular interest in her to me."

Huron looked up at Simon then and held his comments in.

Smiling, Simon raised both his salt and pepper eyebrows. "Besides, I noticed you and Dr. Stuart laughing together quite a bit at the fundraiser. Maybe she actually likes you? Maybe she dates men too?"

"Baba Simon, I think I would like to date Dr. Stuart, but I'm worried that Callia might take it poorly. She doesn't seem to like her much. Maybe I am missing something? Maybe Dr. Stuart isn't what she seems somehow. I know Nik and Emily think the world of her. Maybe Callia is just jealous. What do you think?"

"Well, son, since your parents' death I have really hoped that you would find someone worthwhile to make a life with, to have a family with. I think it would make you happier, much like I think it would help Callia to settle and make a home with someone. I wish you two could make each other happy, but things being as they are, it is probably best that you pursue someone else. I think Dr. Stuart is a very nice young woman, and worth dating at least. I have not noticed anything that would make me think otherwise. Have you asked Callia about it?"

"I have and her answer just seemed so strange. She said something about how Dr. Stuart was fine if you liked judgmental debutants, which makes no sense from what I know of her or what Emily says about her. I think maybe the two had a disagreement over something Callia thought she was the expert on, and Augusta refused to back down or be impressed. As much as I love Callia, she can hold a grudge over a simple difference of opinion." Huron remembered the time Callia hadn't spoken to him for a month, because he had disagreed with her about the fastest way to get food donations distributed to the homeless shelters before the holidays.

"Well, I may have a way for you to learn more of how the wind blows between them, and get something important done for me too." Simon licked his lips.

"I'm all ears, Baba. What are you thinking?"

"I bought an abandoned church camp in the Davis Mountains. I was planning on giving it to Emily for Christmas, to use as a summer retreat for some of the troubled teenagers that she and Dr. Stuart think could most benefit. It was such a good price, though, that I bought it sight unseen. I'm not entirely sure it would suit such a purpose well."

Huron's mind raced to catch up with Simon's machinations. "Would you like Callia and I to go check it out?"

"I planned on asking if you two would. Between the two of you, I know you can tell me the logistical details that should be addressed if my gift is to be useful to Emily and the foundation." Simon nodded and then touched his fore finger to his lips and held it aloft. "But I think it would also be useful if you would take Dr. Stuart along. I think she could help us figure out how many and what kind of professionals would truly be needed at the camp."

Huron smiled with the satisfaction of seeing his plan to keep Callia commitment free work out so well with so little devious manipulation by his own hands. He was certain he could charm Gus enough to make her look fickle in front of Callia, or play charmed enough by Gus to make Callia jealous. He sat back in his chair, relaxed for the first time all day. "No doubt, Baba. I will call them both and beg their help. I think it is an excellent idea."

"Thank you, son. Just remember, you must all keep the camp a secret from your sister or it will spoil my Christmas present to her."

Chapter Twenty

Into the Frying Pan

Cal watched the Texas landscape outside the passenger window of Huron's Hummer go from brown to browner and flatter, as he drove west toward Fort Davis. She sat up front with Huron at Gus's insistence. Cal mulled over that small exchange of words, the most the psychologist had said to her at one time in the last six weeks, since their discontinued kiss. She thought Gus was too quiet in general, so when Huron pulled into a gas station in Fort Stockton and ran in for the restroom, Callia seized the opportunity to talk to Gus alone. She set the nozzle in place to gas the Hummer unassisted and then opened the back door and slid in beside Gus.

Surprised brown eyes met hers, and she resisted the urge to touch Gus. "Hi."

"Hi."

"You're very quiet. Are you feeling okay?"

Gus nodded. "I feel okay. I'm just embarrassed about the last time we talked. I didn't mean to invade your space like that. I'm sorry."

Cal rubbed the back of her neck. "You didn't invade my space, and there is nothing to be embarrassed about." Cal searched Gus's face. "And, I don't think there is anything to be sorry for."

"Cal, I know you don't like me. I know we don't see eye to eye, so I'm sorry..." Gus let her sentence trail off into silence, as Huron returned to the Hummer and popped his head in beside Cal.

"Do you ladies need to use the facilities before we go? It's probably another hour and a half to the camp." Huron laid his hand on Cal's forearm, but made eye contact only with Gus.

Cal watched Gus shake her head. "I'm good to go. Thanks." She smiled at him.

Cal's palms itched. She wanted to send Huron back inside for coffee or something, but knew he would insist she go get it since she hadn't stretched her legs like he had. That would leave him alone with Gus, and he definitely seemed intently focused on Gus for some reason. "I'm good too. Let's roll." Callia squeezed past Huron and concluded the gas pump sale before heading back around to her seat up front.

Huron got into the driver's seat again and turned to Gus before buckling his seatbelt. "I know the scenery hasn't been worthwhile so far, but once we get to the spring at Balmorhea and turn onto Highway 17, I promise it will take your breath away."

Callia swore he intentionally flashed Gus his most charming smile before he turned back around and started the Hummer up again. Her stomach lurched a little, as the large vehicle leapt forward toward the interstate with a roar. Something was up with Huron. He was always charming and nice, but she thought he was making an extra effort toward Gus lately. A voice inside her head that sounded a lot like

Andy teased her, *Yeah, maybe, but what really miffs you is that Gus isn't being nearly as abrasive to his charms as she was to your muddled efforts to play nice.*

"Whatever," she muttered.

"Did you say something, Cal?" Gus asked from the back seat.

"Ah, no, not really. Just muttering to myself."

"Oh."

Gus stared at the back of Cal's head and mulled over their interrupted conversation at the gas station. She was pretty sure Cal was wounded at the very suggestion that there was something embarrassing about their kiss, but she was embarrassed about running out on Cal without any explanation, if nothing else. That was the part she had wanted to apologize for, but it didn't appear that Cal heard it that way. She bit her thumbnail.

As they turned on to Highway 17, Huron used the Hummer's advanced sound system to blast Aaron Copland's *Appalachian Spring* suite.

"Really?" Cal protested.

"What? It goes with the scenery. Gus has never been here before. It makes the introduction to it better. More immersive. More sensual." He shrugged off Cal's glare and tossed a suggestive smile over his shoulder to Gus.

"Thanks for thinking of it." She settled back into the leather seat and let the scenery moving by the window take over all her attention. It was dramatically green and rolling suddenly, punctuated by colorful crops of rocks and slender creeks trickling hints of water that glistened in the sun. Not at all like the flat brown landscape proceeding it. The road curved and tilted and dropped gradually into a valley. Mountains, hazy and purple, played around them barer than the Appalachians of northern Georgia and sharper than those of Guatemala. The northern Chihuahuan Desert did it's best to run as far uphill as it might, browning the feet of the mountains and dusting the horizons beyond the green influence of the valley around them.

Park signs proclaimed Fort Davis and an observatory ahead. "What's Fort Davis?"

"An old army outpost. I think it was mostly active after the civil war. It's a historical site," Cal answered.

"Maybe we'll stop by." Huron flashed her a smile in the rearview mirror. "The fort, the state park, and the observatory are the primary tourist attractions near the camp."

†

The camp turned out to be a slew of cabins, four bunk houses, and a large common building nestled at the end of a long, winding gravel road halfway up a mountain, overlooking the northeastern edge of the Fort Davis park lands.

The cabins weren't particularly posh, but they looked as if they could easily be cleaned and returned to use for housing camp counselors and staff. After ducking into each one, Cal declared the two biggest of them fit enough for their stay, before wandering off in search of the fuse boxes. Gus noted they were the only two cabins that boasted two double beds each. She volunteered to put the sheets they'd brought on three of them, in order to give Huron and Cal more time to get into the grisly details without her, but Huron shook his head.

"We'll each do one, it will go quicker and we might need your input on something."

"I flipped the breakers, and got the AC to come on for both." Cal announced, as she came around from the backside. "Gals in one, boy in the other." She proposed jerking her thumb from Huron to the cabin without any partitioning curtain between the double beds.

"Or I could just sleep on the couch in your cabin. You know, only tax one air conditioner."

Cal laughed. "Nice try, Slick, but I think we can afford to run two of them for a night. Besides, we're probably not that pretty to leer at while snoring anyway."

Gus pulled out a stack of sheets from the Hummer and counted enough to dress his bed.

"Maybe I'm just afraid to be alone in the wild." He mimed a plea.

Cal shook her head and held out her hands for a stack of the sheets that Gus held. "We'll be right next door."

Gus handed Cal the sheets. Their fingertips brushed in passing, and Gus was startled to find that Cal's were cool and smooth despite the heat surrounding them. Her breath gave an involuntary hitch, and things seemed to go in slow motion for several seconds as Cal gave her a goofy grin. Then Cal turned away and headed into the cabin to dress her own bed.

Gus sighed.

Huron held out his hands, palms up, interrupting her train of wanton thoughts. "I could actually use some help with mine."

She handed him a stack of sheets, keeping one for herself. "Oh yeah?"

He blew a sheaf of his fallen blond locks off his forehead and gave a shrug. "Actually, yeah, I haven't made my own bed since I was ten years old."

"Oh. Well, that does make sense." Gus tried to hide her surprise, because it did make sense. Why would someone of his resources make their own bed? Even if he wanted to, his time was insanely valuable when you thought about the cost of hiring house staff per hour versus the cost of his time at work. "I can help."

"You are a lifesaver. Thank you." He smiled at her with the same playful mirth she'd once seen on the face of the amazing Gigante de Cayala sculpture in Guatemala. "I'll help you too, if you like?" His tone was kind and just shy of suggestive.

"I'm probably faster without assistance." She headed for his designated cabin, and he skipped ahead of her, holding the door open for her.

He kept up a litany of lighthearted banter nearly all on his own, which probably contributed to the extra time it took Gus to complete the task.

The screen door bumped behind her, as she stuffed the pillows into pillowcases.

"Really, Huron? You're playing Tom Sawyer with the poor woman." Cal's voice held a touch of derision.

"You're just jealous."

Cal shook her head and plucked up the stack of sheets Gus had left on the table. "I'll make yours. Just try and hurry it up a little, will you guys?" She strode out the door, letting it bang closed behind her on its creaky springs.

They finished making the bed and wandered out of the cabin. Huron gathered his tablet and a couple of clipboards with paper and pens attached from the Hummer. Cal joined them without a word, less than two minutes later. Huron handed her a clipboard. "Ready?"

"Like ten minutes ago." She pulled a vacuum-sealed, stainless steel water bottle from the Hummer's passenger-door compartment and tucked it into the side pocket of her pants.

He nodded and headed down the slight incline toward the first bunk house.

Over the next few hours, Gus trailed the two of them, staying at hand to answer a few questions, but mostly just watching them interact. There was consistently a hint of friendly competition between the two and an obvious, respectful affection; but there was something else too. Something more negative that implied a point of contention, maybe of jealousy. They were both tall, beautiful people who moved through the dusty spaces with cool grace in their nearly matching, high-tech camp shirts and beige hiking pants. The grime wouldn't even attempt to stick to them. In her cleanest pair of jeans and favorite free polo shirt, Gus sweated profusely and admitted her own jealousy of their garb.

When they finally finished their full exploration, Cal pulled them toward a picnic table in the shade of a stand of piñon and juniper. Without a word, she took the water bottle from her pocket and handed it to Gus.

Gus attempted to pass it to Huron first, since Cal had already given her first sips on the last three breaks, but Cal held her hand up like a stop sign. "You drink first. You're the hottest."

Huron giggled. "Yeah, she is," and waggled his eyebrows at them.

"That's not what I meant." Cal blushed so fast from the base of her bared throat to the roots of her hair that Gus worried she would heat stroke.

"I know. I should have bought some new clothes that were meant for this climate." She unscrewed the bottle's cap and took three small, slow sips. Cal had refilled the bottle from the kitchen's tap in the common building, but she still wanted to leave plenty for the both of them. "Thank you." She passed the bottle and cap on to Huron.

He took a healthy glug and handed it quickly back to Cal. "Yes, thank you for taking care of the important details, as usual."

"You're welcome." Cal took a drink, pocketed the cap, and then set the bottle on the table, still open and neatly centered to all of them. She drew her clipboard from under her arm and put it face up on the table between herself and Huron. He set his own down beside hers, with his dark tablet underneath it.

"I think we can keep the prep costs under forty thousand dollars if we start before Christmas and give ourselves until May to finish the work," Cal said.

"That would leave us more money to recruit and hire the staff, at least for the inaugural season." Huron crossed his arms, stepped closer to Gus, and asked Cal, "How many kids, total, do you figure we can fit into a camp here each summer, given our assumptions so far?"

Cal gave Gus a glance she couldn't decipher, so she just smiled back and prompted, "What is a practical number?"

Obviously thinking about it, Cal crinkled her forehead, and a wayward, visceral want struck Gus to kiss her pulsing temple and see if that soothed the crinkle. She shook her head, an attempt to dismiss the thought, but Cal took it as something else.

"Just give me a second." Cal chewed her lip. She paced back and forth a few steps with her head down before coming to a stop facing Gus. "Between four to five hundred kids a summer, assuming four-week sessions for a twelve-week operating season, with four counselors for every bunk house plus the basic full-time camp officers and staff."

"And Harbor House can afford to give that many kids the opportunity to experience the joys of a first-class summer camp, absolutely free, way out here?" Gus questioned. It seemed an incredible boon, a chance to do some real preventative mental health care. They could create an experience that allowed some of these children a unique chance to be themselves and learn in a safe and supportive environment—away from the stressors, like hours alone at home, that normally surrounded their summers. Maybe they could even help some kids realize that just because they were born into a situation, it didn't mean that they needed to stay in that situation.

Huron bounced on the balls of his feet beside her. "Yeah, you know Cal's the queen of logistics, but that number fits with my estimates too."

"What would that include?" Her question was addressed to Cal, but Huron rushed to answer.

"Well, food and lodging, obviously, but also they would get to participate in sports, arts and music, and lots of nature lessons. We could do hikes where kids get to learn about animals, plants, maybe how to set up a tent." He tapped his lip with one finger. "And I bet our supervising psychologist could come up with some social coping, team building, and leadership development activities to give them some extra interpersonal skills to take back home."

The thought of designing those things did give Gus an immediate thrill. She knew she was suddenly beaming. "Oh, I certainly would."

Huron laid his hand over Gus's shoulder. "With a little ongoing support from a few sponsors, the kids might also be able to go on day trips to the observatory, the fort, or the galleries in Marfa." His bright, blue eyes bore into Gus. "I know Emily will do her best to get sponsorships that allow for expenses like that."

Gus nodded at the message he was telegraphing. Emily would need help. She would have to be social and focus some time on fundraising too. "I will help."

Huron smiled and patted her back. Gus recognized that he was exceedingly touchy today. Not inappropriately, but still more in her physical space than ever before, and she wondered if he was feeling emotionally vulnerable over the whole camp idea.

Cal cleared her throat. "I have another idea."

"Oh, on funding?" Huron looked ecstatic to Gus.

Cal rubbed the back of her neck. "Uh, no…"

Huron's face fell and Cal mumbled, "It's probably stupid anyway."

"I'd still like to hear it," Gus encouraged.

Cal's eyes slid sideways toward the gnarled roots of the nearest juniper. "You could invite motivational speakers to visit with the kids. Like doctors—or professional athletes and musicians—who had rough starts themselves, to talk about how they found the courage and motivation to keep trying to go beyond their initial circumstances." As she finished speaking, her beautiful, blue-green eyes lifted to meet Gus's.

"I think that is a fantastic idea." Her mouth went dry, as Cal gave her a small smile. "Thank you."

Cal blushed again but more softly than before. "You're welcome."

Huron stepped between them, arms wildly gesticulating his enthusiasm. "I bet we could talk every one of the San Antonio Spurs into coming out for a few hours every summer, and I go deep sea fishing with a few key Dallas Cowboys I could strong-arm into it too."

†

Touring Fort Davis's historical displays had sounded like a good idea to Cal, given the light in Gus's eyes at the mention of doing so, but Cal quickly realized that it wasn't going to dissipate Huron's weirdness any. He doggedly shadowed Gus's every step, as they walked the parade grounds, pausing for relief in the shaded, broad-board porches of brick and stucco buildings squared up around the flag. For the briefest of moments, she was able to pry Huron from Gus's side by suggesting they enter the maze of the park's museum. Apparently, Gus's determination to read absolutely every display placard in its entirety, twice, was more standing still than he could handle. He was in the far corner made for younger children, trying on re-created uniforms and brandishing a wooden cavalry sword at the cloth dummy created for said purpose.

Cal rubbed her forehead distractedly, willing her building headache to retreat, and peered over Gus's shoulder. The reference to San Antonio swam out at her, and she wondered if that was what had Gus entranced, so she read the rest.

In 1867, Lieutenant Colonel Wesley Merritt marched one of the first Black Regular Army regiments from San Antonio to Fort Davis. The soldiers of this unit later became known as the "Buffalo Soldiers" and served throughout the American west. From 1867 through 1881, Black Regulars were the only troops stationed at Fort Davis.

Cal looked to the display itself and found several very old pictures of young prosperous black families, as well as young black men in full military regalia with proud expressions. Furthermore, there were pictures of women in Victorian garb climbing rocks, and wealthy Latino craftsmen hosting picnics for all the denizens of Fort Davis.

"It was so diverse," Gus observed, as she backed up a step to stand beside Cal. She stood so close that her shoulder brushed Cal's arm.

Peaches. Cal finally realized that the faint, sweet perfume typically trailing Gus smelled like peaches. She smiled. "Typical Texas I think. It was a frontier. So what you could do, what you could make, usually mattered more than what you looked like."

"Maybe. But not the typical experience most of the youth we would send to our camp will have known. Seeing that it does exist, that it has existed for over a hundred years in their state, on any level, will be inspiring for some of them. It will give some of them hope that they can find a way to make a life and look this proud."

Cal tilted her head and thought about it, putting herself in the shoes of a child struggling to stay out of a gang or find someone successful who looked similar to them. She remembered how hard it was for her to find a role model to identify with, even though she was surrounded by wealth and people who looked like her, even though examples of strong, white women were all over television and film. "Yeah, I think you're right."

Gus playfully smacked her shoulder and mocked astonishment. "You just said I'm right."

Cal scoffed. "It happens. I'm willing to admit it happens." Brown eyes met hers and everything disappeared except the whole-hearted smiles they shared. The moment was beautiful. Uncomplicated. It felt like home, right up until Huron literally pushed his way between them.

"What are you gals whispering about?" He wore a charming smile with a mask of curious innocence, but Cal saw through her childhood friend's antics. He wanted to be the center of attention.

Gus smiled vaguely back at him, but her eyebrows were knotted. She tilted her head toward the display. "Just observing that disadvantaged youth might find all this evidence of prosperous, happy diversity in the old west somewhat inspiring."

"Ah." Huron bounced on the balls of his feet.

"I think she's right. It would be good for kids to get multiple chances to visit here each camping season. Exposure to the park's history and outdoor learning programs couldn't hurt either," Cal added, searching out Gus's brown eyes and then feeling way more ecstatic than she thought she should to find Gus beaming at her.

"Oh, using their educational programming schedule here is a good idea too. It might even save Harbor House some money, huh?" Gus replied.

Cal shrugged. "Well, you guys wouldn't have to create as much educational content yourselves, and that might save some on materials, but you'll have to buy into running and maintaining more buses to transport the kids and counselors back and forth from here to camp. The transport expenses are usually way more of an investment than creating and updating educational programs."

"It will take more money," Huron practically sang and placed his arm around Gus's shoulders. He gave her a suggestively conspiratorial look. "I guess we'll have to find a way to make that happen, huh?"

Cal thought he was just being an absolute cheeseball in his efforts to be the center of attention, but still, she discovered she was a tiny bit jealous of the way Gus so gracefully accepted his uninvited violation of her space.

Gus smiled softly and sighed deeply. "Yeah, as much as I hate things like fundraising, I know I've got to push myself to do uncomfortable things sometimes. For the better cause."

"Like playing nice with bozos like Dan Argyle," Cal blurted the first example that came to her mind.

"Yes, like putting up with Dan," Gus said with a cheerful air. "I realize somethings are necessary evils if I want to help build the more systemic solutions that will help kids on a really meaningful scale."

"Exactly." Huron seconded and squeezed her in a one-armed hug before finally removing his arm from her shoulders. He didn't move away from her though.

"I'm a little shy for my chosen profession. I have to remind myself of the higher need to socialize a lot." Gus shrugged and gave a self-deprecating eye roll.

Cal rubbed her chin and felt herself frowning. "You know, I didn't suspect you were so practical."

Gus smiled. "I'm no operations expert, but I try."

Basking in Gus's pert yet sheepish gaze, Cal realized that she might have jumped to too many conclusions about Gus having debutant aims. This revelation that Gus had to push herself to socialize by framing it as a means of helping others fit better with all the times Em, Nik, and Andy had proclaimed Gus to seem so selfless and well intentioned. And at the moment, it definitely felt like Gus was flirting a little. With her.

†

Huron watched Callia frown and grow closer to glowering at them for several seconds after Gus admitted her practicality. Callia's facial expression reminded him of someone trying to process sour lemonade. He tried not to give in to any of his glee and concentrated on interrupting their exchange before anything positive could evolve from it. "So, now that we've established social manipulations are justified, how about we address our very practical need to eat some dinner?"

The question hit its mark, distracting Gus's attention away from Cal before Cal's frown faded into the mildly pleased wonder showing on her face as she now looked at Gus.

"I am hungry. We skipped lunch," Gus replied.

He rubbed his belly. "Yes, we did."

"I'm sorry. This whole thing was my mission. You two just agreed to help."

"Happy to do so." Gus grinned.

He replied with a smile he knew displayed his dimples. "The least I should do is be a good enough host to feed you." He was certain he could charm Gus sufficiently to make her look fickle in front of Callia, or maybe play charmed by Gus to make Callia jealous. Either way, he was determined to put them securely at odds with one another.

"Yeah, okay," Cal said, frowning again.

"Can we stop by the front desk and get some information on their summer programs though?" Gus asked.

He nodded. "Where would you like to eat, Cal?" He watched his friend.

Her eyes flicked to the tiny sliver of space between him and Gus, and her gaze lost its focus. She shook her head and her eyes cleared. "What about the Mexican place on the edge of town?"

Gus asked, "The one with the woman's name and the bright yellow porch?"

"That's the one," Huron confirmed, hoping she would be openly dismissive of the tumbledown place because it was obvious Cal was into trying it.

The smile on her face lit up brighter. "Cool. Andy said that place has amazing tacos, particularly something about chicken tacos with mole sauce."

Cal cleared her throat. "Probably not as amazing as Tenayuca's, but worth a look, huh?"

Huron realized it must be some inside joke, because the two of them were suddenly sharing grins that were more intensely friendly than satisfied his plan. He picked up Gus's hand and threaded it through the crook in his arm. "Right this way."

†

Ten minutes later, they were finished speaking with the park's on-site historian, and Gus was armed with a sheaf of paper detailing the park's educational programs by seasons. Cal watched her shuffle them into order. One of the schedules—printed on thinner, slicker stock than the rest— slipped to the ground at Gus's feet.

Cal bent to retrieve the paper, but as if somewhat horrified at having Cal do anything for her, Gus bent down first and snatched it from the ground. Cal aborted her effort and straightened up again.

Gus gave her a small smile, a blush showing above the collar of her white polo.

Cal started to smile back, muttering, "I...," but Huron pushed between them again, laying a hand on Gus's forearm.

"We should get going." His bright smile was aimed entirely at Gus.

Gus laughed. "Hungry, huh?"

"Starved."

She patted his hand. "Let's go then."

Huron hurried to the door and held it open for Gus, ushering her outside so that she had to pass in front of him. He let go of the door and followed so quickly on her heels that Cal was forced to catch the door's backswing or get smacked in the face.

They beat her back to the Hummer by a good twenty feet.

Huron held the door open for Gus, handed her up, and closed the door behind her.

138

By the time Cal got close, he was already inside the vehicle with his seatbelt on, adjusting the air-conditioning vents to give Gus more of the air flow. He cast a glance over his shoulder at her and gave Gus a wink. "She can't help that she's slow."

Gus smiled and shook her head. "None of us can, when we've had too little to eat for too long."

"Tacos. We need tacos," Cal replied, because she thought she needed to say something. Anything to cover up the spark of hurt pricking behind her sternum. It was bad enough that Huron was acting like a jealous brat, but it was worse that Gus just put up with it so well. Cal knew it was unreasonable to be upset with Gus for tolerating Huron's antics gracefully, but why had Gus seemed unwilling to put up with Cal's interpersonal blunders? She sighed, knowing the answer was probably the obvious. She was not as socially smooth as Huron.

†

For the fiftieth time in a tenth as many hours, Huron blatantly complimented Gus while physically pushing himself between her and Cal. Cal scowled at Gus over his shoulder and practically hip-checked him back, grumbling something incomprehensible.

Gus fumed. She had thought the tension between them would ease up after dinner, reckoning it might be related to their long day and hunger pangs, but it had only thickened into some nearly juvenile dance. It was weird, and she realized they were probably using her to play some sort of strange tug-o-war. Maybe this was just a case of two pretty people using the ugly duckling between them to attempt to win some advantage over one another. She shook her head, fighting back her tears. She would not cry about this. She decided to remove herself from the situation. "I'm going to check out that trail up-mountain."

Huron and Cal simultaneously declared their intentions to go with her. "Wonderful idea. I'll go with you."

"You shouldn't go alone. There's snakes and stuff."

Gus flinched and forced herself to give them both a small smile. "If you don't mind, I'd like the time alone. I promise, I won't be gone more than an hour, and I'll watch for snakes and all manner of dangers."

Cal gave a resigned smile that didn't reach her eyes. "Well, you did survive the wilds of Guatemala without our oversight." She glared at Huron pointedly but said nothing further.

"Yep." Gus walked away and let her thoughts run ahead of her like the tall, white clouds scudding south in the bright-blue sky around her. Leave it to Cal to understand alone time. Gus just couldn't figure out why Cal let Huron's heavy-handed charm push her buttons. It's not like Gus was interested in guys anyway, even if Cal somehow mistakenly believed that Gus thought she had a chance of playing romance in their socioeconomic league. Her subconscious rankled and raised a resonant voice of protest. *And if you weren't using that class distinction as a defensive chip on your shoulder, it would be Callia Alexana that lit your fire, wouldn't it?*

"Shut up," she huffed back and kept walking uphill.

Chapter Twenty-one

Fire Starter

Even with sunset fast approaching, the rocks around them radiated an angry heat that matched Cal's internal seething. "What. The. Fuck. Huron." She jabbed a finger in his chest to punctuate each word, and it had its intended effect in wiping all the sticky, smug charm clean off his face. "You're all over her. What kind of shit are you trying to start here?"

He cast a furtive glance up the hill after Gus, but Cal had deliberately waited until the psychologist was out of view and well out of earshot.

Frustration was clear on his face, as he looked back to Cal. "She's playing you."

This was not the direction Cal had expected him to take in his defense. "Oh? And exactly how is she playing me?"

"She's pretending to like you."

Cal couldn't keep the dark, deep laugh that sprung from her belly from barking out. "Uh. Yeah. Obviously, she is pretending so hard to like me that it just seems like I annoy or deeply offend her principles ninety percent of the time."

Huron pouted.

Cal sighed. "Fine. Pray tell me then, why do you think she is pretending to like me?"

"Duh, Cal." His eyes bulged. "Money."

"Money. Really." She narrowed her eyes.

He nodded, best baby face in place.

Anger seared down both her arms and she clenched her fists. "Bullshit. That woman has zero fucking interest in money and you know it."

He shook his head and clucked his tongue. "Not money for herself, Cal. Money for her work, for the means to help more kids. She would do anything for them."

That gave her pause, for a second, but it still didn't make sense. "No. I don't think she would do anything. Especially not something that went against her core beliefs." Gus was a woman who burned from the inside out with righteous compassion. Even when Gus denied her the benefit of the doubt, or railed against Cal's point of view half-cocked, Gus exhibited a definite undercurrent of fervent compassion. Everyone could see it. Even Huron had, so this was about something else. "And second, why the hell would she be nice to me for money? I'm not even on the damn Harbor House board, and you're the major underwriter."

"Exactly." He smirked. "You're truly more money. Money that isn't already in the game. And she's smart enough to know that even if she can't seduce you into being fiscally supportive, she can please Emily by entertaining you, and that might give her more access to funding through us."

She almost followed his chain of logic, despite knowing Gus's compassionate nature. It wasn't a stretch to believe a psychologist could be smart enough to be that subtly manipulative; but then the dimple of smug surety appeared on Huron's chin. That little facial quirk was his tell. He was bluffing. "No."

The smug-surety dimple crumpled. "What? What do you mean no?"

"I mean no, that isn't it. She isn't playing me, but you are. Why?"

He turned his face aside and stared at the horizon. Giving himself time to change tactics, Cal suspected. She crossed her arms. "And you're trying to play her. Why?"

"I want her to leave you alone." He swallowed.

"I don't think she wants that much to do with me anyway. Why bother?" The sheer tingle of heat that prickled her skin every time Gus stood near made Cal wish reality was otherwise, but she wasn't going to kid herself.

"Oh come on, you can't really be that blind. She's like a damn moth to a flame with you."

"I think you're seeing things that aren't there because you're jealous."

"I am not seeing things."

"I'm not going to argue about it, because it doesn't really matter. I'm not in the best mind frame to date, and if she is a moth to the flame, that darting away was probably her thinking wiser of it. It would be hard for anyone to put up with me."

"That's because you are saving yourself for me, Cal." Anguish colored his blue eyes navy.

She heaved a sigh. There was no pleasure in hurting him, but she could give this sentiment no further quarter or it would hurt him worse. "No. Listen to me. I am definitely not saving myself for you."

"Then aren't you looking for love in all the wrong places, like the rest of us? How come you've never actually brought a woman home to see if she fits in with your family?" A mocking bird shrieked something akin to *Do it*, from the trees downhill.

Cal shrugged. "I guess I think I shouldn't have to look. If it's meant to be, then I'll recognize my match."

"You don't have to look. We match. We're equals. I've spent enough time looking around for both of us. Let me do this for you."

"I should let you do what? Tell me what to do? Dictate who I should love enough to spend the rest of my life with?"

Huron held his hands up. "Whoa. Not that. Let me protect you. If you won't let me be your partner, at least let me help you find one worth bringing home. Don't settle for someone who isn't your equal, just because she doesn't have a penis."

"Too far, that's taking it too far, Huron," she growled. "I've never settled, and you know I won't."

He sighed. "You're right. I'm sorry. I know you won't, and that's the problem. I think it's pretty hard to find an equal."

She didn't say anything. He was right about that at least. Sort of. She thought Gus might actually be better than both of them, which wouldn't make her an equal. "That might be true, but it doesn't mean you can butt in. I don't interfere with your love life."

He hung his head. "I know. I just want to protect you though."

She wanted to say that she didn't want his protection, but she did. She wanted any protection from herself and the hidden pains in her heart that she could find, but she refused to indulge those wants. "I have to do this on my own." And she knew it was true. Emily might introduce her to love, but no one could help her recognize it and be brave enough to chance and cherish it. That part she had to prove she could do on her own, if it was going to happen at all.

"It's been that way since you were little, Cal."

"Yeah, but I've got something to prove now."

"What? What on earth could you possibly have left to prove? You're wealthy, healthy, successful and the apple of your Baba's eye."

"That's not the point."

"Isn't it? Don't you want to be adored?" Huron's expression quickly brightened. "That's it. You want me to admit I adore you. Well, I do, Callia Persephone Alexana. I adore you. You're adorable. You have nothing left to prove. We all know you can do it all on your own. Everything. Anything you want to."

Cal shook her head, sad to break it to him. "I know, Huron. And you can too. In fact, you think you can accomplish me, your childhood best friend as your ideal partner, despite the complete lack of romantic chemistry and all emotional obstacles otherwise. But you can't, and I don't want to be adored."

"Then what do you possibly still have to prove?"

Cal heard Gus's voice, soft and insistent, echoing in her head as they'd argued over the priorities of human health and happiness at that fiasco of a Red Cross meeting months ago. A new realization articulated itself for her as she replied to Huron, "I have to prove that I can love, that I'm willing to let someone love and help me just because they want to."

"Damn it, Cal, that is what I'm telling you. I want to. I can do that."

"No, you can't Huron, because I don't want you to. We don't love each other like that. I can't let you help me with anything. It's always been a competition with you and me to see who can do one better or go one higher; and we love that, but that isn't a good basis for romance and you know it."

"We could learn the rest."

"I don't want to learn the rest with you. I'm a lesbian. L. E. S. B. I. A. N. I want to learn the rest with a woman, whether you and Baba believe it or not."

His shoulders drooped and he rubbed his chin, fingernails rasping against the slight stubble of his five o'clock shadow. "You're serious. I get it. But do you really think you'll be able to find a woman who appreciates, I mean really appreciates, all of the great things you've achieved? Someone who encourages and respects your ambitions like I do?"

"All these years I've spent proving I can achieve great things on my own don't feel so important lately." Cal shrugged. "I don't think I care about that as much as I thought I did. I want to prove I can love a woman more than I love achieving anything, and maybe Gus is the best chance I have of doing that. Even you like her. So why the hell would you cheat me of the chance to find out, if you adore me so much?"

Huron paled and fell silent. "Do you love her?"

"No." She rubbed her chapped lips, because the word tasted wrong on them, like it wasn't the truth.

Huron scoffed.

"I mean, I don't know. It's too early to know, and it probably doesn't matter anyway. I respect her, even though I don't want to. I'm inexplicably attracted to her, even though I don't want to be, even though I don't think she's all that interested in me. I'm constantly worried she doesn't think well of me and that's a first. God, it seems I'm the moth to the damn flame."

"I'll say." His eyes reproached her.

"Honestly, Huron, if you're my friend then don't you think you should respect my right to find out?"

"To stand by and watch while you play with matches and possibly set yourself up for disaster? For what? I found you first, I've known you longer, and I already love you."

Her stomach lurched. "Really? Do you ache to spend hours kissing me?"

He sputtered and his face turned red. His eyes wouldn't meet hers.

"Yeah, I didn't think so. Face it, you love the idea of me as a woman you're proud to be seen with. You love the idea of making our families even more strongly connected. You love the idea of winning over your toughest competitor."

"You should too." He shook his hands at the air.

She shook her head. They'd been back and forth over this for years. "But I don't. Not like that. I love my friend, Huron Tyler, the quirky, charming playboy with his keen business sense and surprising philanthropy. You and I would both hate my adoring, striving to be attentive, husband version of yourself. And regardless, my point is that you should love me enough to not interfere with my ability to try loving who and how I want."

He sighed, and she watched the hope leak completely out of his posture. "I take it you're not flattered by this well-intentioned scheme then."

"The road to hell is paved with good intentions and righteous schemes." Cal quoted her mother.

Huron smiled a little, obviously remembering the source of her quote and all the times they'd heard it as little kids in trouble over some plot. He sighed. "Maybe."

Silence stretched between them, growing from an uneasy truce into a companionable resignation. They communicated without words. She knew, without hearing him say so, that he would at least not begrudge her the chance to find out if her attraction to Gus could be something more meaningful. She thought he also knew that she would always value his friendship. That acknowledgment was written on his face and felt warm in the hand he briefly squeezed her forearm with as he whispered, "Okay."

She circled her finger in the air between them. "I'll tell Gus what was up and that we cleared the air." Neither one of them wanted the psychologist going back to Emily with worried hypotheses about their curious behavior in west Texas.

"I can do it." He looked a bit nervous suddenly.

"I know you can, but I want her to hear it from me. I promise, I'll be kind to your intentions in the telling."

"That'd be good."

"Spoken like a man who knows how to negotiate." She laughed.

He laughed too. "If only. I'd negotiate some sense into you. How do you know she isn't in love with me?"

"Are you serious?"

"Seriously curious."

Cal felt herself blush. "Her kiss says otherwise."

"Now, I've got you. You kissed and told."

"Yeah, well just try and use that as blackmail."

"No promises, Cal. I might."

"I'd rather bribe you to convince Baba that I'm serious, whether I bring a woman home yet or not."

He smirked. "If I was smart, I would just say you can bribe me by giving me details about that kiss, but as your friend, I feel compelled to admit that I'm pretty sure Baba already knows you're serious."

"Why do you say that?" She tapped her fingers on the side of her leg, anxious to know, more anxious than she wanted to be.

Huron's smile was simple and kind. "He told me so, Callia. He said he was okay with it. He just wants you to find someone worth settling down with and to be as happy as he is with your mother."

A tension she didn't realized she carried fell off her shoulders. "Oh."

"Now about that kiss, did it lead to hot lesbian sex?"

"None of your business, ever."

"Probably not, but certainly imagining it is my pleasure."

"Ew."

Huron shrugged and laughed.

Chapter Twenty-two

Baggage to Burn

"What really happened, Cal?" Gus's lips minutely twitched up to one side.

"I told you. He wanted to make me jealous of you so he could get a little extra attention." She could tell that Gus knew that wasn't the whole story, and she didn't know how to deflect without obviously deflecting—not with Gus's deep, brown eyes boring into her, seeming to study her every facial tick—so she left it at that.

Gus tugged at her pony tail, and a wavy wisp escaped near her temple. "Yes, you told me what happened with Huron today. I get it. It's hardly new in the realm of human motivations." Her eyes narrowed. "But why did his behavior upset you so much? You seemed more upset than one weird day's worth of twitty scheming warrants."

Cal was not ready to admit that it pissed her off because she was so damn attracted to Gus; and she really didn't want to mention the part about Huron trying to chase her off and why Cal so desperately didn't like that. Those parts could stay unspoken, for now. She shrugged.

"I know there's more to this, Cal. Something sparked this little drama between you two. What was the first trauma?"

"There wasn't any trauma. It's just the normal tension between two people who grew up together like we did." Her voice cracked on the word normal though, and lost its resolution so that her reply sounded exactly as hollow and false as it felt.

A glimmer of worry, a spark of concern, ignited in Gus's eyes, and the blood rushed in Cal's ears. Gus tilted her head to one side and asked, "Is there something that makes you feel like you have no control over your relationship with Huron? Like he refuses to take you seriously?"

Cal almost replied no, but she couldn't bring herself to lie to such direct questions. No one had ever bothered to ask so directly before. "I don't want to talk about it. I don't want to burden any one with my problems."

"It isn't a burden, Cal. I know you don't want to talk about it. I understand that and you don't have to tell me anything you don't want to, but please realize that sharing it with me is doing me a favor. You would be giving me a gift."

Cal sputtered. "Horse hockey. How could giving you my griefs be a gift?"

Gus smiled and bit the corner of her lip before she answered, "Telling me about your problem is a gift, because it helps me know and understand you better. It's also a sign that you trust and respect me enough to give me the chance to listen to you and keep your confidences."

"But you can't fix it anyway." Cal did not want to be any one's pity project, especially not the pity project of a woman who made her libido roar into hungry life like this woman did. "No one can fix it."

"I can't fix it." Gus's face showed no pity. In fact, an unexpected hardness showed in her warm eyes as she softly replied, "That isn't my job. But I can listen to you, and sometimes that helps. Trying to know you is also my responsibility as a fellow human. Our social circles are connected. I want to know you."

Fist curled, Cal took a deep breath. She thought she would find a new line of protest, at least those were the words she was mentally searching out, but she heard herself blurt, "I was molested."

Gus's expression remained neutral and open, and she waited without saying anything.

The muscles in Cal's neck and chest tensed. "I was molested by Huron's dad, David Tyler."

Gus barely nodded and asked, "Have you ever told anyone else?"

"Once." Cal swallowed against the painful heat rising up her throat.

"I take it that didn't go well."

Cal snorted and then sniffled, trying to disparage the tears she felt prickling up in her eyes. "You could say that. I told Baba, but he didn't believe me. He told me that David loved me like his own children and Baba knew David would never want to hurt me or any child. He said that a word like that meant something very specific, and I probably didn't realize what it really meant to be molested." She gulped for air, as if the words had been stuck in her throat, choking off her breath for years. "He said it was very dangerous and hurtful to spin stories like that. That I could ruin Huron and Emily's lives. My own father refused to believe me, just because he didn't want to believe me." She couldn't meet Gus's gaze. This unbearable secret, so big it chased her father away, might chase Gus away too. That uncertainty sent an ungodly chill down her spine and into her heels. Her hands twitched useless at her sides, and she gasped for more air.

"I believe you, Cal." Her breath came back to her body as Gus repeated herself. "I believe you."

With the influx of air, Cal felt a dry sob shake up between her shoulder blades. Gus's reassurance brought some relief, but Cal found there was more she was compelled to confess. There was more pain. "It kept happening. Every time David could corner me alone in their house, when I went over to play with Huron or Emily, so I stopped going over there. I made up reasons to have Huron and Emily come to our house, but I never told them." Her hands trembled.

"Is it still happening, Cal?" Gus's voice was a calm balm in the black rush of things she didn't want to think about.

Cal felt like she was choking. She shook her head and forced herself to take a long, deep breath before explaining, "It stopped when I was fifteen years old. I think because David had his first heart attack and then a triple-bypass surgery. I guess he wasn't up to it anymore." She gave a bitter laugh. "Or maybe he came to Jesus or something after almost dying. He avoided me from then on, but no one seemed to notice the difference except me."

"Baba still didn't believe you?"

Cal shook her head. "If I even came close to bringing it up in any way, Baba exploded over any little nit he could find, from my supposedly surly attitude to my shameful disregard for my appearance. I quit trying, and now David is dead and it doesn't matter anyway. It would only hurt Huron and Emily to know. It's my problem."

"I'm sorry you have to deal with it, Cal, and for whatever it is worth, I believe you. I'm willing to listen if you ever want to talk about any of it."

Cal nodded and swiped her forearm over her watering eyes. "Thanks. Keep this to yourself." She clenched her fists.

She knew she was begging for Gus's confidence. She'd exposed far more than she was willing to expose already, and she hated begging. She hated this feeling of helplessness.

"Yes, for as long as you want me to do so." Gus's face and voice were neutral, simple, matter of fact.

She sounded like she was just acknowledging that what Cal wanted was obviously reasonable, not any sort of favor to grant. Cal uncurled her fists and wiped her sweaty palms on the legs of her jeans. She felt herself blush, as she worried if the psychologist was now likely to label her crazy.

"So, about the logistics, what else do we need to think about to get this place ready for Em to launch a camp season?" Gus asked and her brown eyes still showed no pity, only acceptance. Cal's confession was fact. Maybe nothing more than something that was acknowledged and left on the shelf for now.

The tenseness in Cal's chest and neck slackened, and she gave a small smile. "For one, who will plan the meals and get all the groceries?"

Gus stared into the space above and to the left of Cal. After several seconds, her eyes refocused and she replied, "It's not supposed to rain."

"What do you mean?"

"Isn't this a desert? Or at least arid land? The postings in the fort's museum said that it rained less than seventeen inches a year."

Cal cocked her head. "Yeah, so?"

Gus pointed over Cal's shoulder.

Cal turned to look and saw a towering wall of black clouds winging northward toward them. In the distant valley, she saw the fierce haze of grey and exploding dust that meant torrential rain was falling to the earth below those storm clouds. "Wow. It must be a supercell generated by that hurricane in the gulf. I thought it was still too far away to cause problems."

"Oh. But it isn't a hurricane, right? Not this far inland, is it?"

Cal turned back to face Gus. "No, it's not a hurricane, just a storm that sometimes comes before and after them around here. But this arid land around us is too dry to suck up the rain as fast as those kinds of clouds can make it. It will probably cause flash flooding along the low points and creeks."

"What should we do?"

"Avoid going anywhere. It will be okay. It will pass."

"And the town?"

"They should be okay too. The creeks are empty and should hold the run-off well enough. We should go inside though." The wind gusted in hard and fast and decidedly cooler. "Getting pelted by rain and maybe hail wouldn't be pleasant."

"Right." Gus turned toward the cabin and marched for the porch.

Cal followed closely on her heels. As she pulled the door open and gestured Gus to go ahead of her, the black sky let loose, pummeling the cabin's porch roof with rain and small chips of hail.

Chapter Twenty-three

Cabin Fever

Inside the dim and rapidly cooling cabin, Gus shivered as she noticed the heat in Cal's gaze. She found herself wondering how warm Cal's hands would feel on the bare planes of her hips. It had taken every ounce of her self-control not to reach out and touch Cal, not to offer some physical concern as her past caught up with her. She struggled not to offer her a hug or a hand, and only managed it so well because Cal had looked so unsure and remote. Touching the victim of physical abuse, no matter how compassionately, unless first invited was a hard no-no anyway. But Cal's gaze was direct and inviting now. The problem with touching her now was that Gus wasn't sure she could stop if she started. And once they quenched this fever to touch one another in any meaningful way, this definite physical pull between them, she wasn't sure it would push either of them to a healthier state of being. Maybe worse yet, what if this fevered attraction wasn't a sign of a deep connection at all but still couldn't be quenched?

The wind howled around the cabin. Cal flipped the light switch for the wagon-wheel fixture dangling above, but only one dim light came on. Gus kept fighting the urge to corner Cal and kiss her until she reached through the baggage and prickly demeanor to Cal's vulnerable center.

"I guess we'll have to make do with low light, at least the air conditioning is still working." Her dark hair was waving out in the extra humidity. Gus wanted to smooth it back for her, and to smooth the stormy seas in her eyes too. *Those eyes really are something,* thought Gus as she watched them go from midnight blue to charcoal grey to Caribbean teal and back again. She knew people whose eyes changed color or tone with the clothing they wore or the light surrounding them, but she hadn't met anyone else whose eyes seemed to color coordinate with their emotions.

"You have more important things to be doing than analyzing me, Dr. Stuart." Cal said, but couldn't quite achieve the fully reproachful tone she intended. She found that strange. She felt like she was falling into Gus's wide, brown doe eyes. They were a beautiful shade of sunlit earth: rich farming soil, honey, caramel, falling leaves, and golden afternoon colors.

Gus blinked. "I, uh, I was just thinking you have very nice eyes, Callia. No analysis. I'm sorry." She cast her eyes down to her own hands.

Something about those words pried at Cal's heart like a hungry child's hands prizing at a cookie jar. She touched Gus's chin. "Thank you, so do you, Gus."

Gus looked up again, and Cal felt a flurry of that impossible desire for this contradictory woman fan up from the pit of her stomach right into her throat. "I'm not sure how or why you do it, but you just get under my skin. Everything about you is so fascinating and so frustrating and so…desirable."

Clearly surprised, Gus only stammered a small, "Oh?" Her face flushed.

Cal swallowed. "Look, all I mean is, we obviously don't agree on a dozen things, but I think we let that color our perceptions of one another too much. Watching you here, Gus, I've learned I can't kill my respect for you. I always have respected you. I wasn't drunk on our first date, and I wasn't late."

Gus looked so small, but stood so poised. Cal ached to touch her, to break down the patchy walls of ego hanging on between them with the direct, invasive pleasure of human touch.

But true to her professional training, Gus only spoke an objective encouragement. "Tell me what happened the night of our date then."

Cal rubbed her cheek. "I was only fifty feet from you at the table, right on time, when I tripped and crashed into a table full of beers. Oh, and a bird shit on me."

Gus gave a small smile.

"Seriously. I knew I smelled like beer and bird shit, so I went inside to try and clean up a little. It made me late, and I was still smelly, but I was only fifty feet from your table. Didn't you hear all the ruckus? Didn't you see anything?"

"Oh my, Cal. I'm sorry. I didn't know, and no, I didn't notice anything." Gus's face pulled into a frown. "I think, I mean, I know a bomb could have gone off and I wouldn't have noticed. My head hurt, and I was already so wrapped up thinking about a patient's problems."

Cal stepped closer and put her hand on Gus's shoulder. "No self-care."

Gus licked her lips. "Yes. You're right. I wasn't taking good care of myself, and consequently, I had no grace and not enough attention to spare for you. I'm sorry."

Cal wanted to say something suave and reassuring, but most of all she wanted to kiss Gus slowly, warmly, repeatedly. So, she did, and Gus kissed her back. Their bodies, so different in character and clothing, somehow magically fit against one another without any thoughtful coordination.

The rain gusted sideways against the cabin's wall in a hellish gust of wind, as Gus put one finger between their lips.

Cal loosened her hold, but their bodies remained molded close together.

"I respect you too, Cal. I always have. I'm just scared."

Warmth that somehow felt blistering and chilling all at once wrapped around Cal's chest. "Me too."

"Oh."

"Yeah." A self-deprecating snort raked up her throat.

"Do you mind if I don't save us both by calling a time-out again?" Gus's hand smoothed over the back of Cal's shirt and came to rest, pressed flat against the small of her back.

"No." Cal's gut twitched, hopeful but hopeless. "Do you mind if you don't?"

"No." Gus's hand clutched at her shirt.

"Then I have no objections."

"We're playing with fire."

Cal didn't answer. She crushed her lips to Gus's again and laid her hands on the planes of Gus's blue-jeaned hips before pushing them up under the hem of her white, Peace Corps polo. When her hands met the soft, firm skin of Gus's curving sides they both jolted at the spark.

They stumbled against each other, pulling off clothing, and halted and hitched back into eager kisses several times before they both stood naked and suddenly shocked shy beside the bed. Gus pulled loose her pony tail, dropping the rubber band to the floor.

With both hands, Cal gathered and smoothed back the unruly waves of Gus's hair. She closed the space between their bodies, bringing their bare skin together, and it smothered all oxygen for several seconds. When she could suck in another breath again, she kissed the top of Gus's shoulder and felt Gus tremble against her. Their mouths met, open, wet, and eager to consume one another.

Cal fell backward onto the bed, pulling the smaller woman tightly on top of her. The sweet weight of her body against Cal's breasts—their bellies, hips, and thighs all meeting became a seething fire of want inside her. The heat burned over her every nerve ending, leaving nothing uncharred by the overwhelming sensation of its path. She was already a burn victim needing balm, needing another kiss. Her own wetness blossomed as Gus's slid slick against her. She clutched at Gus's firm butt cheeks with both hands, opening more of Gus's wetness against her lower belly, as she swirled her tongue in Gus's mouth wanting to be closer still. Gus shuddered and moaned in her grasp. That sensation alone was somehow enough to fire Cal's first rippling orgasm, a flutter hard and tight in her clitoris pulsed into the press of Gus's skin above her, and her own voice echoed Gus's earlier moan.

Gus kissed her eyebrow, her cheek, her chin, and then was nipping tongue-searing kisses deep into her mouth before she let Cal breathe out again.

"I want to be inside you." The bedroom was one place Cal believed absolutely in asking for permission first rather than forgiveness later.

"Yes." Gus's answer was clipped and breathy, a plea spoken against her lips in between their kisses.

She rolled the smaller woman carefully beneath her. The softness of Gus's breasts brushed tingles over the tautness of Cal's chest muscles. She fitted herself perfectly between

Gus's legs, her hand lingering over the delicate skin inside Gus's thigh before teasing her even softer folds.

Gus's breath was ragged, and her body arched into Callia's touch, the insistence of the motion sending a fire raging through Callia's own core. In the dim light, Gus's pale skin glowed peach and light gold. Her brown eyes were dark and endless. Every touch between them spoke to Callia of vulnerability and hope. Her preconceptions about the woman beneath her sparked and blazed away into forgotten ash and nothingness, leaving only an impression of infinite heat and love. There was a definite softness to the lust in Gus's eyes that hinted at love, a love that Callia realized she desperately revered and wanted to coax into a blazing life.

She placed two fingers against Gus's pulsing vaginal vestibule. The slick muscles twitched beneath her touch and Gus's body arched higher, their hip bones grazing and greeting.

Gus spoke her name in a warm, rapid whisper, a prayer of, "Callia, Callia, Callia," that faded into a pure guttural cry of joy, as Cal pressed inside of Gus with long slow strokes. Their gazes were still locked, as Cal felt the height of Gus's climax pull her deeper and tighter.

Gus's taut thigh brushed wet and hard against Cal's clitoris and sent her spiraling into an instant and intense orgasm before Gus's pulsing vaginal wall pounded on to a soft, slack completion.

Cal closed her eyes and rested her forehead against Gus's shoulder. Their skin was hot and wet with sweat and desire, but the tears of joy and incomprehension stung even hotter and wetter behind Cal's eyelids. She felt Gus stroke her hair and graze a kiss against her temple.

"Callia, I want to touch you too."

Cal smiled to herself and gave a soft snort. "Oh, you've already touched me, Gus. You might have to give me a minute to recover first is all." She looked up again, searching out Gus's dark eyes and finding them still a breathless, vulnerable well of emotion gazing back at her. She rolled onto her back, careful not to press her weight too sharply into the smaller woman's body, and gathered Gus against her side.

Gus placed her head into the pillow space beside Callia's head and kissed her neck, her breath was cool against Cal's overheated skin.

Hours later, Callia woke up to the gentle thrill of Gus tracing a caress over the muscled lines of her abdomen. It was dark outside, the rain had stopped, and the air was colder against her skin. They made love again, and then famished, they ate saltine crackers in bed and drank them down with the room-temperature Dr. Peppers they'd discovered in an otherwise empty cabinet over the minifridge. Nothing had ever tasted as good to Callia as the sweet soda clinging to Gus's kiss-swollen lips.

Chapter Twenty-four

Serious Interruptions

Gus's eyes flew open to the sound of pounding on the thin cabin door.

Huron sang outside, "Ladies, ladies, wake up. It's important."

Tangled in Callia's arm in a sea of warm sheets, Gus was reluctant to let reality sink in. She said nothing and wondered if he would just go away if no one answered; but then the door rattled as he tried the knob.

"Come on, Cal. I know you hate mornings, but this is important."

Gus felt Cal's arms tighten around her, and Cal whispered, "Shit. I guess that means we need to answer the door before Mr. Important jimmies the lock."

Gus sighed and snuggled her cheek tighter against Cal's neck and shoulder. "Back to the real world."

Cal snorted a laugh. "Unfortunately."

Gus lifted her head and searched Cal's eyes. There was no doubt she knew Cal better now, and Cal certainly knew more of her too, but that didn't necessarily mean that they were an 'us' or a 'we' now. The baggage and barriers might

163

still be more than Cal wanted to tolerate, or more than Gus herself could endure over the long haul. They needed time to talk, but it would have to wait.

Cal caressed her cheek and settled a warm hand on the back of her neck, never losing eye contact with her.

Gus bit her lip and thought it better to say a little something now rather than risking the wait to talk about it all later. "This isn't casual. Not for me."

Cal kissed her briefly. "Agreed. This isn't casual for me either, Augusta Stuart."

Gus gave a lopsided smile. "Good, Callia Alexana."

"Right, so let's get dressed and take care of Mr. Important. Then we'll talk until we figure out what else this is, in addition to serious."

Gus sat up, and trailed one hand down the long sloping curve from firm breast along to Cal's lean hip. "Right." She forced herself to take her eyes off Callia and search out her clothes.

†

"Finally," Huron proclaimed, as they emerged from the cabin.

Gus toed a loose board on the porch and smiled enigmatically.

Cal wished they were still tangled together in bed for the hundredth time in as many seconds and aimed a full frown of dissatisfaction with the situation at Huron. "What's so damned important anyway?" Her voice was a whip.

"Geesh. Didn't you have any coffee yet?"

"No." She softened her tone, realizing she didn't really intend to flagellate him over it.

He smiled. "Oh, well let's go in and I'll tell y'all while you make a cup."

Cal recalled the still mussed sheets and the obvious shambles of the interior that would give away their extra-curricular activities of the night and hesitated. While definitely the easiest way to clue Huron in again, it might not be the tactic Gus appreciated most. She shook her head. "I'm fine. Just spit it out already. What's the deal?"

"That hurricane in the gulf accelerated and is making landfall on Corpus Christi as a Category 5 in a few hours." His announcement was not what Cal would have predicted.

"We need to get back and help open all the shelters," Gus replied.

Huron nodded. "Yeah, we'll be hard pressed to beat the first evacuees there. The mayor wants every shelter opened. Austin and Dallas are opening theirs too. Everyone along the coast from Port O'Connor to Sarita has been directed to evacuate." His eyes narrowed, and he looked back and forth between Cal and Gus a few times.

Finally, Cal brought herself to answer, "Okay, five minutes to gather our stuff and lock up the cabins. Then we'll leave."

"I've already loaded my stuff and locked my cabin, so I'll attend to the office, cafeteria, and commons." Huron patted Gus's back as he passed by her, giving Cal a shit-eating grin over his shoulder.

She managed to growl out, "Thank you," and then stormed into the cabin.

Gus followed and hurriedly packed away her stuff.

Cal did the same, grabbing their towels and stripping the linens from the bed as she went. She stuffed everything into the dirty laundry bag to drag home. Gus bagged their trash. Within minutes, all evidence of their presence was completely cleared from the cozy space.

She hesitated by the door, and Gus bumped into her back. She put her bags down and turned to face Gus. "It might be a while now before we have a chance to talk about anything."

"I know."

"I'm not the smoothest talker anyway."

Gus smiled. "I know."

Cal laughed. "You say the sweetest things sometimes."

Gus dropped her bags and wrapped Cal into a hug. "I know," she whispered into Cal's shoulder, "you'll have to cut me some slack on that front right now."

Cal held her back, breathed in her scent and slowly sighed out, "I think I can do that."

Chapter Twenty-five

Being Right Doesn't Win You Anything

The total number of evacuees had quickly filled all the previously prepared shelters, forcing the city to go to its backup megacapacity shelter plan to use the Alamodome, and Cal was placed in charge of making it happen. Three days in with too little sleep, Cal looked over the fifty thousand evacuees now clustering the building. Long lines of cots filled with weary people stretched across the floor. She plucked a sandwich from the box on the dolly beside her and unwrapped it. The meat inside was still frozen, but she ate it anyway and knew they would probably have to serve them to the evacuees before they were fully thawed too. She'd organized heavy surveillance, but the tensions on the floor among evacuees were thicker than she had expected. Gus had been right about food and a place to sleep not being enough to stem the tide of grief and frustration. She could feel it growing and starting to overwhelm her own compassion.

She was becoming immune, insensitive to the stories and the brutal reminders of their evacuation. She'd wept the first time she saw medics treating the skin sores an old man had suffered from wading out through toxic waters, but there were too many scared and crying children after a while. Several families had endured traumatic separations at evacuation checkpoints or check-ins at overflowing shelters, and their anxieties were becoming normalized. Cal swallowed the last of her tasteless sandwich and heard an old Hispanic woman comforting a mother with two kids, maybe her daughter and grandchildren. "This is not the end," she said, "This is not the end."

It wasn't comforting to Cal though, because the old woman was right. This wasn't the end. All of these people would need shelter for weeks, maybe months. The surge from Hurricane Dorian, the twenty-fifth named storm of the season, had leveled over fifty-five thousand homes and flooded countless others beyond repair as it swirled over Corpus Christi as a Category 5 storm. Adding insult to injury, it had headed back out to sea before raking through Harlingen and into Mexico as a Category 2.

Yesterday, a teenaged Latina from Flour Bluff had told her a disconcerting story. When the girl had gone to buy up bottled water from a convenience store before the storm, a Guardsman paying for gas there had sneered at her and said, "I can't wait to kill you migrant bitches." The tensions were already high between some groups before the storm, and the response wasn't bringing out the best in anyone, as far as Cal could tell. Last night's grumpy briefing with the city manager, the resident National Guard Commander, and Huron about starting up the bus services to Gus's clinic had also revealed that no one could reach Dan Argyle anymore. Cal suspected he had gone into hiding when the media started pummeling him with questions about why his disaster funds weren't covering as much supply as everyone, herself included, expected they should. She was pretty sure the smarmy bastard had embezzled himself an investment loan or something, not expecting a test of this magnitude to hit them in the last few days of the hurricane season.

The emergency ring tone went off on her cell phone. "Great. What now?" She accepted the call. "Callia Alexana speaking."

"Hey, it's Andy. I'm at the Office of Emergency Management, and the weather guys are saying there is a big thunderstorm heading at us from the northwest. They're about to issue flash flood and tornado watches."

Cal sighed. "Okay, I'll batten up here and stop the buses circulating by until tomorrow morning."

"Good. I have another concern though."

"Go ahead. Let's hear it."

"The mental health services facility is by the river, so I looked up the building's flash flood propensity index. Compared to the predicted river rise I'm looking at on my screen right now, I'd say that building is going to be full of water shortly after this storm hits."

†

When the bus left with the rest of the evacuees, the threat of flooding still hadn't seemed too likely. But the rain was coming down harder and the water was a foot deep in the parking lot. Gus watched the van full of the rest of the staff pull out. There wasn't enough room for all of them, so she and a single nurse named Gretchen had volunteered to wait for the van to return. At the rate the water was rising, she wasn't so sure the van would be able to return. She retreated into the building, the water not yet over the buildings' porch.

An emergency alert sounded off on Gretchen's phone. "The flash flooding advisory is now an imminent warning,"

Gretchen summarized to her, and her freckles stood out against her paling skin.

"I'm guessing that means the van won't be able to get back."

She and Gretchen looked at each other in silence for a few seconds. Gus knew it was time to do something about taking care of themselves, but Gretchen's tiny Ford was too risky in the rising water, if it wasn't already stalled out by the water it was sitting in.

"They don't tell you what to do in the event you have to evacuate the clinic." Gretchen gave a grin and trembled. The power went out.

"We need high ground, and we don't want to be trapped in this building." Gus knew from her experience with storms in Guatemala that this was the most important thing in a flash flood.

"We're too close to the river. I don't think there is high ground." Gretchen's voice sounded smaller and thinner as she spoke this time, and she wrapped her arms around herself.

Gus tried to look closely at Gretchen but couldn't see her well enough in the building's dim, backup lighting. She was worried the nurse was scaring herself into a shock. "It's okay. I'm going to step outside and look around for any potential help or safe spots. I'll stay within arms-length of the building. Will you try to call the transportation office while I do that?"

"Yes. I will. Be careful." Gretchen seemed to draw strength from having a task to focus on.

A plan can help sometimes, Gus thought, *even if it isn't much of a plan.* She carefully cracked open the shelter door and pushed her way out against the water now covering the porch. It seeped in the door opening and kept the door from closing fully behind her.

†

The rain was so thick that Callia couldn't see very far ahead. Sheets of grey water blew sideways at her, soaking her jeans and shirt, seeping into her boots until she sloshed around inside of them as well as through the rising water around her. Soon the water would top her boots anyway.

"Gus," she called into the storm.

No answer.

"It is too thick to see anything through the rain, and too hard to hear over the wind," Lieutenant Lindeman shouted from a few feet behind her.

She turned back to look at him. He was standing on the hood of the National Guard's tan Hummer in his effort to see better, but apparently it wasn't helping him much. He hopped to the ground and sludged his way to her side.

"I've got five hundred feet of climbing rope in the deep-water rescue kit. We could use it to tie me off, and I could start a walk out to look while you keep me anchored here and guide me back," he suggested. His military-issued rain gear whipped spastically against his lean form. She noticed the Lieutenant's dark-brown eyes were more uniformly one color than Gus's, and she rubbed her suddenly aching chest as she thought about it.

"Good idea, but you're bigger, younger, and stronger, so you anchor and do the guiding. I'll go out at the rope's end."

"Okay," he agreed. After a minute of rummaging in the Hummer he emerged with the rope and formed a sliding loop that he affixed over her shoulder. "Ready?"

"Ready," Callia confirmed, and the Lieutenant belayed her then fed her slack as she slid her feet out forward through the water in front of her, searching for unseen holes or obstacles before putting her whole weight forward for each next step. Every five steps, she tried calling out to Gus again.

Just as she started to lose hope and wonder if she was even headed toward the building after all, she heard a voice answer her. "Here. I'm here."

She stopped and stood still. "Where?"

Water splashed in front of her, and Gus came into view, struggling toward her. The water was above her knees. Her hair was plastered to her head in a dark, matted mess, and Cal thought she was the sexiest woman alive. Gus faltered and flung her hands out for balance.

Cal surged forward and pulled the smaller woman into her arms. She was pale, wet, and shivering but cognizant enough to return Cal's embrace. "You're okay," Cal rejoiced and repeated.

"Cal, how?"

"How what?"

Gus tugged at the rope crossed around Cal's shoulder and over her torso. "How did you get here? Why did you risk this? Wait, never mind, that isn't important. We have to get out of here now. Oh, and we have to take Gretchen. I've got to go back for her." Gus jerked in Cal's arms, but she didn't let go.

She couldn't stand the idea of letting go.

"Cal, we have to hurry. We have to get back to the building to get Gretchen and get back out again before this water rises more."

"Just Gretchen? She's all that is still left here with you?"

"Yes. Come on." Gus rotated in her arms, leaving Cal's grip around her in place, and pulled them back the way she had come from. Cal followed her, and the Lieutenant, unseen behind them, played out more line. It was difficult to judge how far they shuffled before she saw the building, but Cal suspected they were about to run out of rope. A freckled,

172

redheaded woman with very wet blue scrubs clinging to her wide hips appeared in the open doorway on the porch. Several inches of water were already in the building. They wouldn't get the door closed again.

Gus called out, "Gretchen, grab my hands."

The nurse stumbled forward until she clasped Gus's hands. "We're okay. Hold on to me. I'll hold onto Cal, and Cal will follow the guide rope back out."

Gretchen agreed, and Gus turned slowly in Cal's arms. Gretchen's hands firmly grasped Gus's shoulders, and Gus looked up at Cal with expectant eyes. "I'll hold onto your jeans. Take us out."

Cal forced herself to let go of Gus and turn around. Gus's hands quickly clutched at her jeans as promised, two fingers wrapped through the empty belt loops at each of Cal's hips. The water continued rising around them, and Cal worried it might be too high for the Hummer even before they rolled out. She gave the rope three hard, frantic tugs, signaling the Lieutenant to pull in the slack and guide them back.

They trekked the distance like one hungry caterpillar, in a hurry but bound to slowness by their collaborative struggle through dirty water, the gritty debris swirling around them, and the rain's angry lashes. There had to be less than five hundred feet to travel, but it seemed to take way too long. Cal tamped down her rising panic by glancing down to reassure herself that Gus's pale-fingered grip was still the force twisting at her jeans. She pushed on and trusted Gus to make sure they hadn't lost Gretchen.

The movement of the Lieutenant's body reeling in rope and drawing them closer finally made him visible. His tan gear and the tan Hummer were easy to lose against the dirty river surge and smeared skies. Cal realized that she should have thrown Day-Glo safety vests on both him and herself before they sped away from the Alamodome. "Too little too late," she chastised herself, secure that no one would hear it in the weather anyway.

The Lieutenant touched her shoulder, tugging free the rope. "Is this everyone?"

Gus let go of Cal's jeans and answered him, "Yes."

"Good. Everyone get in then." He flung open the backseat door and pushed them all in before racing into the driver's seat. He shoved it into gear and pulled them out of the flooding lot.

Cal didn't even bother with her seatbelt, and she didn't pay much attention to Gretchen, who perched equally wet and shaky on the other side of Gus. As the Lieutenant steered the Hummer a circuitous route on higher streets back toward the Alamodome, Cal unabashedly held Gus tucked up against her side.

†

"Hey." Cal walked into the tiny inner office, where Gus perched on a cot toweling her hair dry. They were wearing matching Red Cross volunteer t-shirts and jersey shorts, the dry clothes reserved for refugees who needed them, while their personal clothes were cleaned and dried.

Gus admired Cal's long legs in the short shorts. "Hey yourself. You definitely wear these shorts better than I do."

"Hmm. I don't know that I agree, but I'll take the compliment." Cal sat down on the cot, beside Gus, their legs touching.

"The flash flood rages on, I suppose." Gus tossed the towel over the back of the office chair closest at hand. Two of Cal's laptops and her smartphone lay charging on the desk.

Cal rubbed a hand down her face. "Yeah, they expect twenty inches of rain before it all finishes sometime tomorrow."

"And the rivers were already high."

"Yes."

"We're stuck here then?"

"At least until the rain passes and the water recedes."

"It's crowded."

"Max capacity."

"But you have this one cot available." Gus clasped Cal's knee.

Cal put her hand over Gus's. "I do."

"It's a little narrow for two."

Cal shrugged. "We can hot bunk. You can sleep in it the first eight hours, and I can sleep in it the next eight."

"You have a lot to do."

Cal nodded. Her stormy blue eyes grew darker. "I screwed up, Gus. I almost got you and Gretchen hurt."

"We're fine."

"I should have realized that place was too close to the river."

"No, Cal, we maybe should have realized it, but you know we can't plan for every contingency."

Cal sighed. "Yeah, I know. You're right. But this scared me."

"Whoa. Hold on. I think this is the second time you've said I was right, which I'm pretty sure means the earth is about to open up and swallow us whole."

Cal snorted. Light returned to her eyes. "It gets worse. I think you're right a third time."

"Now, I am flabbergasted."

"I'm serious though." Cal intertwined their fingers. "Mental health care should have been a higher priority for these folks, and I should have organized things so that your

175

services were more easily available. Some of these people are in shock."

"Yeah." Gus scooted back on the cot, leaned back and opened her arms. "As are we. I think we need a few minutes, and I would like to spend them holding onto you."

Cal glanced at the cot. "Well, even together we probably still fall short of the three-hundred-pound weight limit on this thing." She eased herself back and settled into Gus's hold. "I can spare a half hour."

Gus pressed a slow kiss to the top of Cal's head, and closed her eyes with a sigh. "This is even better than being right." She felt a laugh ripple through Cal's body, and Cal squeezed her tighter.

Chapter Twenty-six

Safety in Numbers

Gus finished her rounds of the Alamodome, satisfied that she'd at least given something to the most desperate families. The last three days without any area designated for mental health services or buses running anywhere had passed in a haze of doing a lot, but never enough. Despite knowing she was probably too tired, hungry, and emotionally wrung out for her own good, Gus refused to let Cal take her home for the day. "I need to find Dan Argyle and find out what we can do to get mental health services back in action tomorrow. Too many people need the help."

"You can't help anyone if you work yourself to death." Cal crossed her arms and glared at her, as they stared each other down in an empty utility hallway.

She was relieved to finally have a moment alone with Cal. They still had not found a chance to have the talk she wanted to have, the one about what else besides serious this relationship between them was going to be, but just seeing Cal was reassuring. It re-energized her a bit. "I'm fine. I can go two more hours and that will go a long way in getting things set up again."

"Bullshit. I'm not fine after all of this and there's no way you can be either. You're going to hurt yourself toughing it out. We can get to my house. Let's go home for the evening. You can call Dan to work out the details from there, after we've had hot baths and a hot meal."

"I might not be able to reach him by phone the first several tries, Cal. It's better if I start trying now." And she wasn't sure she could stay cognizant after a hot bath. She desperately wanted to go home with Cal and do nothing more than curl up into a never-ending cuddle, as she slipped into oblivious sleep for a dozen hours. In a real bed, no less. But then she would find a million reasons to let the plans to get mental health services back online slide to another day. "I have to see if I can reach him. Why don't you go home? I can use the cot in the office when I get too tired."

The look on Cal's face was just shy of furious. "You're so stubborn." Purple smudges underscored her eyes.

"How do you think I ended up on a blind date with you?" Gus expected her smart retort to lighten the mood, but as she watched a thunderstorm of emotion gather in Cal's eyes, she realized her intentions backfired.

Cal gnashed her teeth and hunched her shoulders. The vein just beneath her jaw pulsed with more vigor. "How many damn dates did you go on?" Her blue eyes were electric ice in their sudden ferocity.

"I went on a lot, too many, but it wasn't—" Gus started to explain herself, but Cal interrupted.

"You're so damn intimidating." Cal stood straight.

Gus didn't fail to notice how intimidating the tall, slender, all-business woman could be herself. "Me?" Gus blinked. "I'm intimidating?"

"Yes, that is what I said." Cal pointed a finger at her. "You. Are. Stubborn. And. Intimidating."

Gus tilted her head to one side. "In what way do you find me to be intimidating?"

"It's not just me who finds you intimidating. You are intimidating. First off, you have a doctorate in psychology. All shrinks are intimidating, because the rest of the nonshrink world doesn't know when you're assessing and judging us."

She couldn't keep herself from correcting Cal for some reason. "I'm not a shrink. Shrinks are psychiatrists. I'm a psychologist."

Cal scoffed. "Fine, you're a psychologist. Who appears to be competent, caring, and helps a lot of people according to Emily—which probably means that you've seen a lot of crap and are even better at seeing through bullshit than the average schmuck. Then there is the whole Peace Corp thing, and the socially and environmentally sensitive things, and the Red Cross volunteer thing. You're an unassailable goody-two-shoes. Third, you're always so damn sure of yourself. You state your opinion like fact, and you never look scared or wrong. And since you never talk about yourself, I mean really talk about yourself and your insecurities, it appears as if you're either perfect, want to appear perfect, or think you're perfect...but then again, you're so damn polite and calm, it is a safe bet you don't think you're perfect, which only makes you look more perfect. You never appear to need to vent, or cry on anyone's shoulder, or just take a bleeding time-out for Christ's sake. Oh hell, you know what I mean. Aren't you ever lonely or scared?" Her voice was an exasperated whisper. Rough from lack of sleep, overuse, and agitation.

Gus felt her bottom lip start to tremble, and she focused on the ground as she tried to reign in her own emotional response, knowing they were both too tired.

"Surely, I'm not the first person to ever tell you that you're an imposing person?" She heard Cal ask.

"I...you...yes, you're the first person to say that. You're the first person to mention being upset about me not talking about my own insecurities. For that matter, you're the first person not related to me to ever ask how my day was and look like you really wanted to hear a response." Gus felt herself tearing up. She sniffled. "Callia, I am alone. I am lonely. I am tired. I'm not at all sure what I want. I want my family. I don't want to burn out. I want to make the clinic here a success. I want metal health services to be available for more people. Some days I feel like I'm pushing a rock uphill alone, knowing the rock is going to be pushed back down as soon as I get close to the top...or there will be some big hole I can't push the rock past alone, and I won't be strong enough to hold in place long enough to accumulate any help pushing it." Gus's breath became too ragged for her to keep talking. Her chest hurt. Her vision was blurring. Her throat was tightening. Her face was hot. She could recognize herself having a first-ever, bona fide panic attack, and she couldn't do a damn thing about it. She shivered, and cried.

"No, no, no, Gus. No, honey. Please don't cry. I'm sorry. I'm sorry." Cal's breath was in her ear. Cal's arms were wrapped around her, pulling her in tightly. Gus gave in. She tucked her head into the warm crook between Cal's graceful neck and shoulder. She took a deep breath and let it out slowly.

Cal held her. "I take it all back. I'm not sure what I said to break down your walls, but it wasn't worth it." She stroked back the fine hair at Gus's temple, and murmured mundane reassurances against the top of Gus's head.

"Fmdgtbe," mumbled Gus after several minutes.

180

"Hmmm?" asked Cal loosened her hold on Gus ever so slightly. "Are you okay?" Cal's voice sounded thicker than usual and quavered.

Gus nodded against her chest before leaning back enough to meet her eyes. "Forgive me, please." Gus rearticulated, but she didn't move to detach herself any further from Cal. Instead she squeezed Cal back for a second, a simple hug. "And thank you, for—" Gus started.

"Don't mention it. My pleasure," Cal interrupted.

"I…I'm glad." Gus smiled a bit. "Uh, we need to talk, but can I stay here while we do it?" Gus implored, indicating her space inside Cal's arms.

"Hmm, hmm."

Gus marveled up at Callia's blue eyes, noticing they'd morphed into this wonderfully comforting shade of chambray and twilight blue.

Gus took a deep breath and started, "Okay. I am alone. I was alone, and I wanted to do something about it. I knew I needed friends, a social support system, someone to share myself with in this new place, especially while trying to do something as hard as starting up the clinic. That is why I went on that Internet-dating service, and why I endured so many dates, hoping to find and build friendships. I didn't go on so many dates because none of them were good enough. I went on so many because I couldn't let myself open up. I presented my opinions as fact, and probably looked judgmental and hypocritical, because I was so scared and tired. I wasn't ready. I mean, I didn't have an open mind about it, and maybe I didn't even have the right reasons for dating. I knew it. That is why I'd given up, and I never should have agreed to meet you when Emily insisted on it. But it was Emily, and I knew she wouldn't play matchmaker lightly. I knew she was trying to help, and I wanted to please her, and I dismissed my own issues as inconsequential for the time being. And then, because I wasn't ready, Callia, I messed up with you. I dismissed you, and blinded myself to who you really are, because I was attracted to you, and I wasn't ready."

"And now?" Cal asked, and squeezed her briefly as if to remind her they were still embraced.

"Now, I know I don't need you to love me. I have friends and a social network in you, Emily, Nik, Huron, and Andy. I have already found what I need to be happy, but I still want you to love me. I want another chance. I want a chance to love you."

Cal kissed her slowly before replying, "So far as I can speak to your wish Gus, consider it granted. I would also like to request a redo."

"Why?"

"I complicated it all with my baggage too."

"Everyone has baggage, Cal. I know better than to hold that against anyone. I should have given you the benefit of the doubt and let you explain your own behavior without passing judgment."

"I was guilty of giving my preconceptions too much weight too, Gus. I let my own insecurities get to me, and it was making me more bitter and sarcastic by the day. I had a bad attitude about anything my best friends tried to do to help me. I want another chance too. I want a chance to love you. I think this spark between us is pretty damn serious. What do you think? Can I have permission to find out?"

Gus found herself hot and cold at the same time. The energy humming through her veins and singing in her chest wasn't panic anymore, it was hope, and she held the door to her heart wide open. "Permission granted."

"Great. Then I'm taking you home. Right now." Cal smiled. "We'll save the world some more tomorrow, I promise."

Chapter Twenty-seven

Better Laid Plans

At first, Gus was petrified when Cal announced they had a meeting with Huron and her father. Even though they had planned the return of mental health services together, better laid plans for everyone this time, Gus knew Cal didn't need her to present those plans. She wasn't sure why Cal had insisted her presence was so critical, until they were seated across a boardroom table from Huron Tyler and Simon Alexana.

"I'm not sure why you two care about the details of our plan so much, but since Harbor House is allowing its supervising clinician the time to organize and run these services for the Red Cross, I guess you have a right to know more about them." Cal jumped in feet first and apparently ready for some sort of controversy.

Realization dawned on Gus at about that moment, so she hurried to explain, "This new plan has a more realistic and sustainable long-term schedule for me. For us both, really. I'll have more time to see my existing Harbor House patients once the plan is in action, and it will be easier for Cal to arrange for families to make use of mental health services on site without having to involve me every day."

Cal nodded. "And there won't be any need to run additional facilities or manage as much transportation with four roving, rotating teams of mental health professionals visiting the shelters and community centers on this schedule. I assure you that we can keep up services for the displaced families for six months, with minimal impact to Harbor House's new clinic."

Huron smiled like the Cheshire Cat. "I'm sure it is a sound plan, Cal, but what money are you going to use to staff these rotating teams?"

"The Red Cross will supply funds." Cal bit the words out with more certainty than Gus felt. Despite that being the purpose of one of the funds Dan Argyle oversaw, he had already turned down their plan and suggested that the funds just wouldn't be available for at least another two months. He vaguely claimed that operational expenses in Austin's few shelters had far exceeded expectations, and he'd had to make an inconvenient executive decision about how to support them in the shortfall.

Huron snorted. "Not from what I hear. They won't have the money available for at least two months."

"Then I will." Cal folded her arms over her chest and fixed a glare at Huron.

"That's a lot of money." Gus was shocked.

Cal shot her a conspiratorial grin. "Yes, it is, but I'm good for it, and I can beat it out of Dan Argyle later, if I need to."

Gus expected Huron to object. After all, according to Cal, he had tried to sell the idea that Gus was someone after their money once before. Maybe Cal didn't bring her along to defend her labor hours or priorities. Maybe she was here for moral support? Maybe she was supposed to object? "And if he doesn't endorse the Red Cross paying you back or taking over the expenses you'll risk just losing every penny of that."

"One person risking the entire sum is too much risk." Simon Alexana spoke for the first time outside of greeting them before they sat down.

"I don't care. It's just money. I have it, and this is the right thing to do." Cal's hands fell to her knees. Her jaw jutted out.

"Let us help you do it, Cal." Huron's face was grave and probably unconsciously mimicking Simon Alexana's expression, Gus observed.

Cal shook her head. "I don't know that it's the best use of your money. I mean, I know it's a good use, a good cause," Cal glanced to Gus, "but what if there is a worse need? We might need to pool our personal finances to donate more for something the Red Cross isn't supposed to help finance at all."

Huron shrugged. "We'll find a way if it comes to it then, but this is the problem now. You're the one who usually says to put out the fire in front of you first."

"Then you believe this is that important? Or do you think Gus is somehow manipulating me to be a cash cow and that you need to protect me?" Hot, angry energy crackled through Cal's question and in her eyes.

Huron glanced at Simon, sighed, and then placed his hands flat on the table. "I don't think Gus manipulated you into this. I do believe it is vitally important to these families, and more importantly, I believe that even if I didn't side philosophically with y'all's plans to get mental health services back in action that I should still be willing to back you up because you're my family."

185

Simon coughed. "We should be willing to back you up just because we love you, not because we do or don't believe you're right."

"What? Since when?" Cal's voice rose half of an octave and dripped skepticism.

Huron pointed a finger at her. "Now don't start, Cal. I know you're angry at Dan, but don't take it out on us."

Simon patted his shoulder. "And we know we haven't appeared as supportive as we want to be. We believe in what you and Gus are trying to do for these dislocated families."

Huron ran his hand through his hair. "Yeah. Look Cal, I know it's a little hard to believe, but I've taken some things to heart lately. I've always prided myself on being able to accomplish anything I set my mind to. At some point, I started to see giving up anything as a weakness. I thought of us as deserving wealth and success because we earned it, and on some level, I guess I thought that love should be earned through manipulation and effort like everything else."

Cal huffed. "Well, I'm glad you finally figured out what I've been trying to beat into you for years, but what the hell does that have to do with this?"

"You are so not touchy feely." Huron snorted.

"Never claimed to be."

Gus clasped Cal's hand under the table. "But deep inside you are, Cal. I think they are trying to tell you they want to help because they love you," she interjected and hoped it didn't backfire.

Cal looked confused. Her question was a whisper, as she glanced back and forth from Huron to Simon. "Really?"

Simon nodded and smiled.

Huron replied, "Yes, that is what I'm trying to tell you, thick skull. You were right, when you said about how we have to prove we can let others love us even when we're not doing anything to earn such affection, sometimes even when we're asking for help. Or in this case, a couple hundred thousand dollars." He gave a lopsided grin. "Let us love you. The way you want to be loved this time. Let us help you and Gus."

Mouth slightly agape, Cal looked intensely at Simon.

Simon's eyes were teary. "*Kopelia mou*, I am proud of you. I want to do this because it is right, because it is within my power to help, and because I love you."

Cal's tears fell silently, tracing wet trails that gleamed on her high cheekbones.

Simon cleared his throat. "I love you, kopelia mou, and I hope you will find it in your heart to let us help you and Gus do this."

Gus squeezed Cal's hand.

Cal sniffled and replied, "I love you too, and so I will try *Babaki mou*."

†

Sleeping at Cal's had quickly become a custom in the last two weeks, and Gus was glad that night was no exception. She was still reeling from the flurry of meetings, budgeting, and recruiting tasks they'd flown through as a consequence of their agreement with Huron and Simon. She watched Cal discard her skintight jeans for a pair of baggy, blue, bamboo pajama bottoms, and sighed at the warmth of want growing in her belly. "You know it really isn't fair for someone with such gorgeous legs to also be so competent and cerebrally gifted."

"Competence is the ultimate sexy, Doctor." Cal glided over to the bed where Gus reclined, already ensconced in an oversized and threadbare Duke University t-shirt. She sat next to Gus, propped against the brass headboard. "And that is probably why you're so damned attractive too, so you can hardly complain."

"That was uncharacteristically smooth, Miss Alexana." Gus knew her face-splitting smile had to be more goofy than sexy at the moment.

"I'm learning." Cal laughed and grabbed her hand. "I'm also trying to learn how to take care of you, so tell me why you are sitting in my bed looking so pensive, when you could just be lecherously leering at me." Cal's thumb rubbed softly over the edge of her hand.

"I'm not going to lie. That meeting, all of today's developments, mostly scared the bejesus out of me, but at the same time, it's sort of a relief."

"Oh yeah, how so?" Cal kissed the top of her head.

Somehow that kiss felt more intimate and full than some of their most searing and passionate kisses. Gus leaned her head on Cal's shoulder and wiggled closer. "Well, it was good to see Huron and your father support you, of course, but I think it was also because it reinforced that I really do have a social network here. Emily, Nik, Andy. Even Huron and your father jumped in and started helping us, me included, as if I belonged."

"You do. You have a social network."

"And you."

"And me."

"I've made friends, deep and abiding friends. I have a rich social life here."

"And you don't even need to keep going on bad dates to make new friends." There was a warm and lovely possessive undercurrent beneath Cal's teasing tone.

Gus laughed. "That is a huge relief."

"So what else were you so cutely contemplating in my bed?"

Gus looked up. "Cal, what does *kopelia mou* mean anyway?"

Cal grinned. "It is old Tex-Greek for my little girl."

"Oh." Gus lean against Cal's shoulder again and kissed the back of her hand. "It's definitely still Greek to me."

Cal groaned.

Chapter Twenty-eight

Where There is Smoke

Outside, the first cold front was arriving in San Antonio with a wild toss of dust and russet colored leaves. Curled up on Cal's sofa, Gus breathed in the steam from her chai latte and watched Cal pace the floor.

Cal finally paused in front of her. "Here is how I think it works. Dan has started and runs at least four small charity organizations that I know of. There are several instances in the donation data, where an individual makes a donation, like say a hundred dollars, to something specific, like the Hurricane Dorian Relief Fund, on the condition that Red Cross send half of the donation on to another specified charity that is, in fact, one of Dan's charities."

The smell of cloves and cinnamon tickled Gus's nose, as she took another sip of her tea before asking, "Why would Red Cross even agree to that in the first place?"

"Several legitimate reasons, but the most usual one is because the smaller charity did some of the grunt work in soliciting the donation in the first place." Cal's forehead puckered into a frown of concentration. "Or maybe, because the charity has agreed to do some small part of the relief work for the Red Cross."

Over the last two months, as they'd grown ever closer—so close that most of Gus's clothes were already in Cal's closet, if she was honest about it—Gus learned that she really loved being the one that Cal talked things over with. She grinned and asked what she suspected was the obvious question, "So, passing part of the donation to one of Dan's charities could be legitimate then?"

Cal smacked the back of her right hand onto the open palm of her left and then spread them both in acquiescence. "That part probably is, but the part where one of Dan's charities then issues a twenty-five-dollar relief check back to the original donor, or one of their close relatives, probably isn't." She shook her head.

Gus sat up. "But why would the individual put in one hundred dollars' worth of dirty money in order to get only one quarter of it back as clean money?"

"He wouldn't. He would put in say thirty dollars to get twenty-five back clean, expecting Dan to profit the five-dollar difference."

"So where does the other seventy come from?"

"Dan provides it to them, because he knows it's going to cycle back to him in a few weeks with an extra five dollars attached to it. Let's say he borrows fifty dollars from one of our regional Red Cross discretionary accounts and adds twenty dollars of his own money to total seventy dollars. He gives those seventy dollars to Joe, then Joe adds those seventy dollars to his dirty thirty dollars and puts it into the donation channel. A day or so later, Joe donates one hundred dollars to the Red Cross on the condition that one of Dan's charities gets half. A week later, the Red Cross channels the "new" fifty dollars to Dan, since he is the regional director, but he puts it back in the discretionary account. The Red

Cross forwards the other fifty to one of Dan's charities. A few days after that, Dan's charity sends Joe's brother, Bill, a twenty-five dollar grocery card, and that leaves Dan with twenty-five dollars, which is five more than he loaned out in the first place, using his money."

"Not that I condone it, but it's five dollars," Gus pointed out and sipped her tea.

"Yeah, if it was only one instance of a one-hundred-dollar donation, but what if it was a thousand instances of a thousand-dollar donation?"

She did the math in her head as she rested her empty tea mug on the side table, and then froze where she sat. "Then he would earn fifty thousand dollars."

"Yeah."

"Shit." Gus could feel her eyebrows migrating higher in surprise.

"Yeah." Cal gave her a baleful grin beneath dark eyelashes.

"But you could never prove that unless you could see all of those accounts plus who the donors and the beneficiaries were at all of the charities." Gus bit her lip.

"Exactly. Which is highly unlikely to ever happen, and that makes it a perfect scheme." Cal heaved a long sigh.

Gus's mind raced around the various implications, until she found one stickier than the rest. "So how do you know about it then?"

Cal hung her head. "Because I'm curious and nosy and have access to data that can be cross-referenced to see it."

"And you can't just anonymously drop a report on the right desk at the IRS or the FBI?"

"I could, but none of the authorities would take it seriously as an anonymous audit report. And since me looking across organizations at that data violates all of the contracts we have with those charities and some privacy laws, then I would have to be willing to pay the price for presenting it with my name on it."

"Oh. I see." Gus chewed on the side of her left thumb and mulled it over some more.

Cal sat down beside her and fidgeted with the frayed edges around the hole in the knee of her jeans.

"Why did you look at all this anyway, Cal?" Gus wondered if this was grudge-driven behavior, and she didn't want to jump to conclusions about Cal's motivations, given how much grief that had caused both of them on their blind date so many months ago.

Cal sighed. "I'm a bitter bitch, and I hate Dan Argyle."

"Did you want to find something to burn him on?"

"Maybe. Probably. But not just that."

"What else?"

"I wanted to figure out why he refused to use any of the discretionary funds to support our mental health services and social work plans back in October. I thought I would find some sort of political reason, like maybe one of the other funds or one of his charities might be a pet cause. I thought that his reasons might be smarmy, and I could, at least, be snarky about it." Cal folded her hands in her lap and looked up at Gus. "But I didn't think I'd find evidence of anything illegal."

"And now that you have?"

"It drives me crazy that I can't do anything to fix it. And worse, I don't think I'll be able to get anyone to believe me." Her breath shuddered, and she swiped a hand over her teary eyes. "Just like with David Tyler."

It was the first mention Cal had made of David Tyler since hurriedly confessing to Gus in West Texas that Emily and Huron's dad had molested her. As with any patient reliving aspects of a traumatic injustice, Gus felt an overwhelming surge of empathy for Cal, but it was backed by very new and very visceral anger. "I think I can help." She took Cal's hand and held it.

"I know. I know I need help processing it or grieving it or that psychological stuff."

Gus stifled her laugh. "Well, maybe, but I can't do that."

Cal startled, "You can't?"

"Number one, I'm a child psychologist, and although you're precocious, you still don't qualify as my client population of expertise. Number two, it isn't ethical or wise to try to work with those you love."

"You said love." Cal's voice wavered.

"I did."

"You love me." Bright, blue awe toppled into triumph over the cold grey fear in Cal's stormy eyes.

Remembering all of that time she had wasted denying Cal was special, Gus's stomach wrenched. "I do love you."

"I love you too."

The size of Gus's smile felt like it might crack her face. "This isn't exactly how I imagined us saying this for the first time, but somehow it's still fantastic."

"Yeah, and you're right, you did just help me." She leaned in and kissed Gus.

The revelation of love and the warm intensity of Cal's kiss, gobsmacked her, but eventually she remembered that she had another point to her original offer of help. "Cal?"

"Hmm?"

"I also meant that I think I can help you get Dan to give himself away."

"Wait, what?"

"Well, if you wire me up and I get him to tell me about it, would that give you enough evidence to go to someone in authority?"

"Um, first of all, there isn't any need to wire you up. They have button cameras and such these days."

"Oh, cool," Gus replied, leaving the differences in their affinities for gizmos unspoken.

"No, no that's not my point." Cal smiled widely. "Sorry, I'm still a little light-headed from the kiss. My point is, or rather my points are, that it could be dangerous and difficult and I'm not sure if it would prompt any authority to do anything anyway."

"Oh."

"Besides, how in the hell would you manage that anyway?"

Gus laughed and couldn't resist saying, "I'd use my dark magic in persuasive psychology."

"That's a thing then, huh?"

"Not exactly, but I can apply some basic principles from psychology to get most people to open up about most things, given enough time." Gus shrugged. "Maybe I can get Dan to say something compromising. I wouldn't push it to the point of putting myself in danger."

Cal rested her elbow on her knee, her chin in her hand, and took up the classic thinker position.

†

The edge of the black plastic button hidden in the cleavage line of Gus's bra rubbed her breast sore, but the physical discomfort of wearing the digital recorder made it easier for her to play the role of frustrated co-conspirator. Her low-cut black oxford and skintight jeans made it easier for her to think of herself as the racy schemer she needed to be to convince Dan Argyle to help her. She put both hands on his desk and let her pain show. "I hear you can help me, but I'm not sure I can trust you."

"Of course, you can trust me." His eyes traveled over her chest and down toward her hips before coming back to meet her gaze.

"I don't know, Dan. I mean what I'm about to tell you is not exactly nice. I've been a very bad woman, and I'm not sure I believe you're as understanding about my vices as others have hinted you could be."

He scoffed and chuckled, making a poo-pooing gesture with one hand. "Come on, how bad can you be? You're a child psychologist."

"Well," she bit her lip, "let's just say, hypothetically, that I made some unsavory contacts during my Peace Corp days, and that they entrusted me to launder large sums of drug money when I returned to the United States."

His eyes opened wide and his mouth went slack.

"See? You're horrified."

He shook his head and stammered, "No, no I'm not...I just...why would you do that? Hypothetically, I mean?" He licked his lips.

She drew a deep breath. This part was even harder for her to say, but she had to make herself look far worse than she suspected he was behaving. "Let's face it, Dan, child psychologists put up with a lot of snotty kids and shitty parents without making much money. There is never enough money to fund our damn clinics. If we go into private practice, then we make a little more money, but we're stuck dealing with even snottier kids and shittier parents. They just happen to have more money. Soon, we're just as burned out and jaded as a homicide investigator. The drug dealers are going to find someone to launder their money. That's just reality, right?"

Dan nodded emphatically. "Yes."

"So, I don't see anything wrong with that being me. Hypothetically, that is. I mean, if I make it safer for them, then I keep more kids from getting involved in petty laundering schemes and getting hurt in the process. Plus, I make a little more money, which is fair and keeps me from burning out so quickly. I can pass a little more money on to clinics and charities of my choice."

"But how do you do that?" He leaned forward across his desk, smiling encouragingly at her.

"Well that's my problem, Dan. I don't know. I'm not good at this sort of thing, and I don't know anyone who could help. Do you?"

"What if I told you that I could help you?"

"Gosh, I would just be so relieved and so grateful, but how? And why would you be willing to help someone who has been so bad? Someone like me, who would be breaking the law?" She fixed him a stare with all the desperate interest she could muster.

†

"I can't believe he told you all of that." Cal tapped the space bar on the keyboard, pausing the three hours' worth of video.

"I can't believe he showed me all of that." Gus was wide-eyed in the dimmed room.

"No shit." Cal couldn't keep the devilishly satisfied grin from spreading across her face.

"Is it enough?" The top buttonhole of Gus's black oxford was still gaping, revealing the smooth swell of each breast above her black bra.

Cal licked her lips. "I don't see how it couldn't be."

"But I lied."

"Like a rug on fire." Cal grinned again.

"Not helping, Cal." Frowning, Gus drew in a deep breath and let it go slowly.

"Sorry. I just can't believe how the softhearted Dr. Stuart totally kicked ass with her dark magic." She stood up and pulled Gus into a hug.

"It's not exactly the most ethical application of my education." She leaned her forehead on Cal's shoulder, and the fall of her russet hair hid her face completely.

"No, but do you still feel like the ends justified the means?" Cal rubbed one hand slowly over her shoulders and kissed the top of her head. The thought of Gus feeling guilty produced a surprising stab of anguish in Cal's chest.

"Relatively, yes. I have to pay the piper, though, and explain to the authorities why I lied so blatantly for such devious purposes."

"Does it bother you though? I mean will you lose sleep over this?"

Gus lifted her head. "I'll be okay. I wouldn't have taken on these pangs of guilt if I didn't think the cause wasn't worth it. I just have to let everyone in on it now, so to speak." Her face was calmer and smoother, as she looked into Cal's eyes.

"Including Dan?"

"Yes, and more importantly, Andy, Emily, Huron, and your father."

"I get telling them Dan was crooked, but what does it matter to them how you determined that?"

Gus touched her cheek and smiled grimly. "It matters to me. Telling them how I found out, what I was willing to do, reveals more of who I am to them. And because I love them, they deserve to know me."

A moment's fear gripped Cal's belly. "What if they don't believe you?"

"They might not." Gus shrugged. "After all, how did you put it? I'm an unassailable goody-two-shoes?"

Cal felt herself blushing. "Yeah."

198

"Well, regardless, it doesn't matter if they believe me. You were right. It matters that I tell them. That they know I'm not unassailable, and that my goody-two-shoes intentions have limits."

The silence settled around them for several minutes, as Cal kept Gus held in close and thought over it all. Her voice sounded distant and tinny in her own ears as she told Gus, "I think I need to tell Emily and Huron about David."

Gus's hands were cool on her face. Her kiss was sweet, soft, and warm on Cal's lips. The world righted itself again, and Cal's voice was stronger as she explained, "I have to give them a chance to know and understand me too."

"You know, I used to think that falling in love with someone who wasn't already perfectly boring and content, someone who might have some unresolved emotional baggage of her own, would just further deplete my reservoir of compassion and empathy." The bottom lip of Gus's smile trembled ever so slightly.

Cal ran her fingertip over it. "And now?"

"I think loving you re-energizes me. With you, my love and my willingness to let you love me is enough. Enough to give me a better perspective."

"Enough to help us conquer the traumas?"

Gus nodded. "And to remind me that there is something that burns even brighter, a happiness that remains as keen and immutable as an eternal flame."

Cal arched one eyebrow. "Please don't start singing that Bangles song."

"Just because you remembered to say please, I guess I won't." Gus giggled.

Chapter Twenty-nine

Three-Alarm Fire

Emily sat next to Huron on Cal's sofa, with her hands tucked in her lap. They waited expectantly. *Now or never*, Cal thought and forced herself to start talking. "I have something to tell you both. It is very difficult for me to say it, and it will probably be even harder for you to hear it."

Huron giggled. "Ah, don't be scared Cal. We already know."

Cal shook her head and clenched her fists so tightly, she could feel her fingernails digging into her palms. "I'm serious. Whatever you think I'm going to say isn't this. I've never even hinted at this. I've always been scared it would destroy your lives."

Emily's mouth gaped, and the mirth fell from Huron's face in less than a millisecond. "You're a little scary right now."

"I'm more than a little scared." The air conditioner kicked on and hummed in the brief silence. "I'm trying to ease into this. To break it to you gently, but I'm not good at that sort of thing."

"Just do it, babe. We know you. We don't expect smooth," Huron said with a half smile.

Cal took a deep breath for courage and then plunged into her worst nightmare. "Your father molested me." She braced herself for denial, unsure if it would be angry and adamant, mocking and dismissive, or silent and skeptical, but certain there would be denial. She tucked her chin to her chest reflexively, protecting her vulnerable neck, and she didn't need a psychologist to analyze that and translate it into an indication of fear.

Huron's face was instantly of a pallor similar to a dead frog's belly. His eyes were glazed. "Oh, God. Oh, God. You weren't the only one."

Cal's head snapped her chin from her chest of its own volition. "What?"

Emily was visibly crying. Her lips were compressed stark white.

Frown lines etched Huron's face, depriving his good looks of all youthful appearances. "Little Jill Beckford." He swallowed. "I walked in on him. When we were about fifteen years old." He shook his head, unable to continue.

Cal's mind churned. When they were fifteen, David had suddenly stopped molesting her. She narrowed her eyes. "What did you do?"

Emily sobbed. "I'm so sorry. I'm so sorry."

Cal remembered Emily had been Jill's babysitter that summer. The Beckfords had moved away from Alamo Heights just before school started up again.

Huron put his arm around his sister and hugged her close. "I stopped him. I took Jill away from him. I took her home. Dad had a heart attack." He shook his head. "I didn't know. He swore it was only Jill. I made him get help. I made him make sure Jill had help."

"No one told the police," Cal stated, already hating that their social status made this an expected norm.

"No," Emily admitted, looking miserable. "No one told the police."

"I couldn't, Cal. I didn't ask anyone else not too, though. But he wasn't a bad man. He was a sick man, and in this disgusting sickness he hurt others." Huron rubbed his face. "I guess I just fixated on trying to make everyone better." His hands shook.

Something else clicked into place for Cal. "That's why you started Harbor House."

He nodded.

Emily spoke, "We didn't know, Cal. We would"—she hiccupped— "I would never have risked letting him near you. I would not have let him get away with that."

"But you let him get away with it because it was Jill." Cal wanted to be angry. She reasoned she had a right to be indignant.

Emily shook her head. "I didn't. I never let him forget it."

Huron added, "We never let him think he'd made enough amends for it. I think we punished him for it more than the courts would have." He left unsaid what they all knew. David Tyler could have, would have, bought the court's leniency. And in the interest of protecting Jill, the whole legal system would have done its best to keep the whole thing away from the press.

Instead, Cal reasoned, they'd done the best they could as teenagers to try to make good things come of it. Not just for David and Jill, but for all those facing similar woes in San Antonio. They'd never stopped either, even after David died, and even though shame never threatened the family. Emily and Huron had kept expanding Harbor House. First financing care for the underprivileged through local, private practitioners, then building shelters for the abused. Now, when there wasn't enough private care to meet demand, they'd opened Harbor House's own mental health clinic for kids.

Emily stood up and approached her, small hands clasped in a trembling plea. "Please, Cal. Forgive us. We didn't know."

"I know." Cal sighed. "I didn't tell you. I didn't give you a chance." She hugged Emily. "I'm sorry."

Emily just hugged her back.

Cal kept hold of Emily for the moment and looked to Huron. "Did you tell Baba?" She had to know if her own father had continued to deny her to protect his best friend. If so, she wasn't sure she would ever be able to forgive him. She tried to swallow the lump of ire growing larger in her throat.

Huron shook his head and a lock of hair fell across his forehead. "I'm sorry. I couldn't bring myself to tell him. I couldn't."

"I tried to tell, Baba, but he wouldn't believe me." Cal couldn't keep her tears at bay. They fell down her face, as Emily clutched her tighter and apologized again.

Huron stood and dropped his gaze to the floor. "That's my fault too." He shook his head. "I'm sorry. I didn't know that not telling would have that kind of effect on you or Baba." Tears tracked down his face when he finally met her eyes again. "I'd lost my dad, in a way, and I guess I needed yours. I needed you and Baba to love us still, and I was afraid if I told y'all that you wouldn't."

Cal's heart unclenched. Her father hadn't known any more than her lame and scared admission. She could see that believing her would have been a shock, and this was just further proof of what he had told her then. The accusations would have destroyed Emily and Huron's lives.

"We were afraid of losing you." Huron's voice was barely a whisper.

"You know better."

He looked up at her.

She held open an arm, and he rushed in to hug her and Emily to him. She knew better now too. Her whole family loved her, and they weren't perfect. As messy as a three-alarm fire, they were warm and real and they brightened her life. Forgiveness felt like flying.

Chapter Thirty

On Three Conditions

Gus stood watching, as Cal served piping hot tamales to the last family in line at the Tyler-Alexana Holiday Helpings Event. The sun had long ago set on them, but the party patio on Tyler Groceries' corporate campus was filled with laughter, and the river below shown with the holiday lights from the cheerful décor. It was a moment of mirth that Gus knew these remaining refuge families desperately needed.

Cal placed the serving tongs into the nearly empty chafing dish and turned a dazzling smile on Gus. Gus felt her heartbeat play triple time. She leaned in on her tip toes, definitely shorter than Cal in her sneakers, and pressed a lingering kiss on her lips. When she finally stood down and opened her eyes, she found that Cal's were still closed. A dreamy smile rested on her face for several seconds before she opened them and asked, "What was that sweet distraction for?"

"I was just having a moment of gratitude."

Cal's blue eyes sparkled and danced, as she took Gus's hand, linking their fingers. She opened her mouth to say something, but didn't get started before Lorina Alexana startled them both. "I've been waiting to borrow you girls."

"Oh yeah, how can we help, Mom?" Cal grinned and squeezed Gus's hand, telegraphing that there was something to get back to in their gratitude conversation.

"Your father wanted to take a minute with the family to give thanks."

"Oh." Cal cocked her head. "Okay."

Lorina smiled and beckoned. "Well then, come along."

Cal stood rooted, looking at Gus.

Lorina chuckled softly and pulled on Gus's free hand. "That includes you, Gus. I for one am most thankful that Callia finally felt free enough to fall in love with you and share you with us." She stared at her daughter until Cal accepted the warm authority in her mother's eyes, such a mirror of her own.

"I, too, am extremely grateful to have found Callia, and to be so welcomed by this family," Gus answered, and Cal let go of her hand with a soft parting squeeze.

Lorina tucked Gus's hand into her arm and led them toward a cluster of trees by a stone dock on the river. They appeared to be the last to arrive. Nik winked at her, as Lorina released her hand and they came to a standstill, finishing out the group circle of glowing faces in the golden landscape lights. Over the last month, Gus had been lucky enough to meet the older siblings, Hans and Coen, and their families. She smiled to them where they stood near their father, with their arms around their respective wives. Their return smiles emphasized Lorina's earlier sentiment. She felt welcomed by this family.

She was glad to see the cluster of family included Andy and his fiancé, Mina. All of the kids huddled near a camp lantern at the picnic table, sharing some game on a tablet. They whispered and giggled advice to Mina's oldest son, as he took his turn controlling the game. The cool Texas winter night was a velvet curtain around them. Oak limbs creaked and swayed above head, some of their dry leaves still shivering and lingering.

Simon Alexana cleared his throat. "It is the time of year when we are grateful to have family, and even more importantly to me, the time of year that I am proud and grateful to have family that does so much to care for each other and our community. I have come to realize this year, as we've welcomed so many struggling families to take refuge in our city, that I do not express my gratitude to you enough. I realize that I have been so wrapped up in my own expectations that I failed to fully appreciate all my blessings. I have made even graver mistakes at times, that I am sure have caused you to doubt how much I love each of you." He looked expressly at Cal before continuing, "I am grateful that you all are gracious enough to forgive and love me anyway, and I am grateful that you still trust me to love each of you. I decided that I should take this chance, while we are all together, to tell you that I truly do love and appreciate each of you." His eyes shined in the dim light, blurry with tears, and he sniffled. "I appreciate your compassion. I am grateful for my family, and I thank God for you." His face was full of love as he gazed explicitly at his only daughter.

Huron placed a hand on Cal's shoulder. His expression was harder for Gus to read, but his voice was level and sincere as he replied, "I am grateful for these things too, Baba. I am happy to have you in my life and happy to call your family my family. I thank God for you."

Emily clasped Gus's hand and squeezed it as she announced, "And I am thankful to see our family bigger and stronger than ever. I thank God for this grace."

"Amen," said Andy.

†

Underneath the wide limbs of a white oak wreathed in white lights, Cal pulled Gus closer and kissed the top of her head.

Gus leaned her whole body against Cal's and whispered provocatively, "So, you led me over here to have a momentary make-out, huh?" She pushed her hand inside Cal's swallowtail jacket, luxuriating in the softness of her black cashmere sweater and the sharp intake of breath her touch elicited.

Cal's abdomen tensed, and she stutter-stepped back by half a pace, shaking her head. "Um. Not exactly. I mean, we should talk first." Cal smiled. "But then the make-out part does sound good."

A snort of laughter escaped Gus. "Okay, so talk first. What's up?"

Cal toed the ground, plucked at a thread on her sleeve, and glanced back toward her family clustered by the river. "I would be an idiot if I didn't propose to the one woman my family accepts as perfect for me. I mean, shit, I'd hear no end of it if I was too lazy to keep this romance burning."

Everything in the world but Cal's face faded from Gus's focus, and her heartbeat pounded in her ears. "Um, was that a proposal?"

"Oh, God...I just.... Damn, Gus, I'm so, so sorry. I meant to make that...uh...way more romantic."

Gus gave Cal a look.

Cal swiped her hands down the front of her jeans and visibly swallowed. "What do you think?"

"About?" As far as Gus was concerned, this was the one and only time she would ever entertain anyone's proposal, so she wasn't about to make it easy.

Cal cleared her throat. "Marrying me. I mean would you want to?"

"I think there are three conditions before I answer that question conclusively. The first of which is that you really ask me, intentionally, Callia Persephone Alexana." Gus smiled.

"Right." Cal nodded and the left corner of her lips turned upward in a sly half smile. She kneeled on one knee and reached inside her left boot. She pulled out something clenched so tightly in her hand that Gus couldn't even glimpse a hint of what she held. Cal clasped one of Gus's hands with her own empty hand and cleared her throat. "Augusta Manda Stuart, you have taught me the importance of trying to see others as they are and not how I hope for them to be. You make me feel loved just as I am and challenge me to be comfortable in my own skin. You reward me repeatedly with your own appreciation of my love for you. I know we are very different people, but we are equally competent. I think our love gives us both a greater potential for happiness together, as partners in this life. I would like to share everything with you from here on out. I promise, I will choose to grow our love each and every day if you will marry me."

"I can think of no greater honor and no greater joy, Cal, than to be your wife."

"I'm so glad." And her expression did look particularly, physically relieved.

Gus tilted her head and squinted at the beautiful woman kneeling before her. "Why do you seem so especially relieved?"

"Well, carrying my great grandmother's ring around in my boot all the time, trying to get the nerve up to ask you, was starting to really chafe." Cal opened her clutched hand to reveal a ring of delicate gold filigree set with a fine cushion-cut sapphire.

"Hmmm, I see. Well, you know my consent still depends on two more little conditions."

"Oh, yeah. I forgot about your conditions, in midst of all this emotional butter fluff. I guess my second asking was sufficiently appropriate to meet your first condition?"

"Yes. Very well done. You may stand."

"Thank you." Cal rose, still holding onto Gus's hand. "And your second condition is?"

"A big Texas wedding."

"But...."

"No buts about it, Cal. We'll need room for at least three hundred people to attend. My family alone will take up a hundred spaces, what with my aunts, uncles, cousins, parents, siblings, nieces, and nephews. And I still need to invite my closest friends from my Peace Corp days, graduate school, and my fellowship, so that will be another fifty or so. And then there are the fifty or so friends I made through San Antonio Matches4All."

Cal pulled a long face and her lips twitched sideways, as her eyebrows furrowed into a minor scowl. "I draw the line at Michelle Wynne. That woman is way too into you."

Gus laughed. "Okay, so maybe not all of the dating service friends, but still two hundred on my side alone, or we'll have to have it in Georgia."

"Okay. I get it. We have to have the wedding in Texas, or we'll cause the other hundred guests my mother will invite to have coronaries. A big Texas wedding it is. There's a historic train station on the other side of the convention center that just might hold enough people."

"A train station?"

"It's pretty. I swear."

"It doesn't matter. Everyone will be looking at how beautiful my fiancé is anyway."

"As if." Cal blushed. "Anyway, what's your third condition?"

"It's more of a wish."

"What's your wish?"

"Is it too soon to talk about kids?"

Cal coughed and then laughed. "Well I wasn't expecting that one, but no, it is not too soon to talk about kids. We should probably come to some agreement on that one."

"Yeah," Gus prompted.

"Right, well, they scare the hell out of me, but I want two of them."

"Me too," She admitted, surprised they agreed without debate.

Cal looked shocked too. "Really?"

Gus nodded. "Yeah, and I'd like to have one of them."

"Me too," Cal insisted.

"You would? You would like to be pregnant?" It was more than Gus could imagine at the moment.

Cal frowned. "Not exactly. I mean I'm sure I will hate being pregnant, but I know I'll find you adorable pregnant, and it only seems fair that I return the favor."

"Hmm. I'll be scared for you," Gus said.

"I'll be scared for you, too, but I'm older so I get to go first."

"How do you figure?"

Cal grinned. "What do you mean how do I figure, Dr. Stuart? You're a smart woman. I'm closer to forty than you are, so my child bearing days are more limited than yours. Simple as that. I'll go first and test it out. Do you think your younger brother would consent to donate the sperm?"

Gus sputtered, "Whoa, whoa, slow down Ms. Alexana. I know you're a logistics queen, but let's have the wedding first."

"All right, fair enough." Cal shrugged.

"But do you think Nik and Emily would be okay with Nik donating sperm? I mean I would want my baby to look like you."

Cal laughed so hard she snorted. "Yes, Gus, I do, and I understand. I can't imagine a baby more lovable than one who looks like you."

"Then I have a definitive answer to your question."

Cal clutched the ring between her forefinger and thumb in her left hand, and held Gus's left hand with her right. "Oh, you do, huh? Then what is it?"

"Yes," she replied, "I will marry you, and I promise to learn how to love you better every day, for the rest of my days."

Cal slipped the ring on her finger.

About the Author

Lacey Schmidt

Lacey Schmidt holds a doctorate in industrial-organizational psychology that has afforded her many opportunities to travel and learn how all kinds of interesting people help make the world go around. She resides in Houston with her wife, and they find the cheaper cost of living there very convenient (given their penchant for expensive hobbies like photography and scuba diving). Previous publications include a poetry book, *The Nightshade Lexicon*, the short story "Love's Luck," and the novels *A Walk Away* and *Catch to Release*, published by Affinity Rainbow Press.

Lacey's website http://laceyschmidt.blogspot.com contains free poetry, art, essays, and music.

Lacey's Internet Presence:
http://laceyschmidt.blogspot.com/
http://www.amazon.com/Lacey-L-Schmidt/e/B00P71M0QO
https://soundcloud.com/lacey-schmidt
Twitter: Lacey Schmidt @shrinky_schmidt
https://www.facebook.com/laceylschmidt

Lacey Schmidt

Other Books from Affinity eBook Press

Changing Perspectives by Jen Silver
Art director, Dani Barker, lives life on the edge and finance director Camila Callaghan thinks it's necessary to stay in the closet to maintain her position. When Dani and Camila meet, they both sense an attraction, A change of perspective for both women is needed if they are to reach this goal.

Death is Only the Beginning by JM Dragon
What would you do if you were in a fatal accident with a stranger and ended up in heaven with them? Only to find out it wasn't an accident, it was murder. Follow the ghostly adventures of these two acrimonious strangers, who help two women find love and find closure for their predicament.

Shotgun Rider by Ali Spooner
Kim and Laney, sweethearts for fifty years go on a road trip to their childhood home state of North Carolina. They follow trails they made as younger women, and relive cherished

memories of their lives together. A haunting story, of romance, and lifelong friendship.

For the Love of a Woman by S. Anne Gardner
In a world where oil is supreme, passion rules reason and there is always the threat of civil war. In this jungle of power Raisa Andieta resides as one of its masters. Her only desire is to rule it alone. Carolyn Stenbeck is just trying to keep her marriage together. Her only desire is to be able to escape and never look back. When Raisa and Carolyn meet, it is like fuel and fire…A storm is brewing. Civil War is in the air, and passion like the coming storm begins to erupt.

Dress Blues by Dannie Marsden
Lucinda (Luce) Velazquez had it all; a job she loved, a woman she loved, and a bright future ahead of her. In a flash of light surrounded by the sound of twisting metal, her life changes dramatically. Her inability to share her deepest thoughts and fears threaten all that she holds dear. Can she allow her lover and others in or will she lose it all?

The Bee Charmer by Ali Spooner
After the death of her father, Nat St. Croix needs to decide on which direction her life should take. Does she continue her life alone, as a trapper and trader, or does she start over and try to fit into a town surrounded by strangers? Will the call of the wild and all that is familiar or, will the call of love capture Nat's heart?

We're Not in Kansas Anymore by Annette Mori
Silver Lining, a successful lesbian romance writer, is just starting to come out of the dark tunnel after her wife's untimely death when she has the crazy idea to sponsor a contest. Silver has more than an unwelcome stalker to

overcome as she struggles with the guilt over her attraction to Jasmine and the lingering memories of her dead wife. In this prequel to, The Review, learn where it all started.

The Organization by Annette Mori & Erin O'Reilly
The feisty, fiery women from Asset Management are back for another heart-stopping adventure! This time, their sites are set on a new mob boss Leonid Petrov. Val is tagged as the go-to member to infiltrate Leonid's inner circle. Tasked with keeping Leonid's impossible new wife, Gina, safe, Val encounters more problems than solutions. Will wild card Gina be Val's Achilles heel and lead to her demise, or will it fill her with a strength she didn't know she had?

Jeager's by JM Dragon
When your world turns upside down and all your safe secure yearnings are thrown to the wind what happens? What would you do? University lecturer Dr.. Kirsten Van De Pelt shortly due to retire early from her academic life is about to find the answers to those questions when Corley Anders, a TV star, enters her life. Will Kirsten take an opportunity of a lifetime or simply settle for the safety net that has been her life.

Running From Love by Jen Silver
Sam Wade returns home from a business trip to discover her wife, Beth left her for another woman, Lydia. To take her mind off the breakup, Sam accepts an assignment to learn to play golf at the newly opened Temperley Cliffs Golf Resort in Cornwall not knowing that is where Beth and Lydia plan to go too. There is more than one way to run from love; from never having to make a commitment and say those magical three words, "I love you." Find out what happens when they

find themselves together—sport, betrayal, jealousy, and love form an unforgettable fusion of emotions.

Specter of Fear by Erin O'Reilly
Anne and Bailey are in love and planning a future together. Only the letters that Anne keeps getting are filling her with fear and doubt. Could the love they share really be a sham? Or is there something more behind the letters? Is the sender of the letters after Anne, Bailey or both women? Find out in this suspenseful tale…or is it a real story?

Back in the Saddle by Ali Spooner
The crew from *Cowgirl Up* are back in the saddle for more fun. In their new adventure, Coal, Stormy, and Gene get the chance to be part of something they have always dreamed of—a cattle drive. Even without the gang being at the MC2 ranch, there's still plenty of action going on with a new addition, Doc Bo, brings a hint of jealousy and maybe the start of a new romance. Pull on your boots and hats, and hold on tight as you ride along with the crew of the MC2.

Faith in Rayne by Dannie Marsden
Welcome back Rayne and Lisbet from *Rayne Comes to Town* and *Rayne's New Beginnings*. Their life has flourished since meeting. Rayne ventures to Telluride, Colorado, where both adventure and trouble land at her feet. Lisbet heads to Telluride to reunite with Rayne, her head filled with dreams of their future only to have her dreams come crashing down. Can she find the strength to fight for Rayne, allowing her faith to guide them back to their love?

Affinity
Rainbow Publications

ebooks, Print, Free ebooks

Visit our website for more publications available online.

www.affinityrainbowpublications.com

Published by Affinity Rainbow Publications
A Division of Affinity eBook Press NZ LTD
Canterbury, New Zealand

Registered Company 2517228

www.ingramcontent.com/pod-product-compliance
Lightning Source LLC
Chambersburg PA
CBHW071152260626
47162CB00003B/1013